MARIE-HÉLÈNE LEBEAULT
AUTHOR OF THE EVERS SERIES

# THE QUEST
## —— FOR THE ——
# PHANTOM
# FEATHER

DEFENDERS OF THE REALM - BOOK THREE

First edition
Ebook: 978-1-7390278-1-0
Paperback: 978-1-7390278-0-3
Hardcover: 978-1-998386-29-1

Editing by Rachael Lammie
Proofreading by Alli Wait
Cover by Miblart

BEACHES AND TRAILS
PUBLISHING

# About the Author

Marie-Helene Lebeault lives in Quebec, Canada and is the mother of two young adults. A retired teacher, she now spends her days writing, translating academic manuals, and lending her voice to corporate training videos. She enjoys reading, hiking, and going to the beach. She is also an avid rollercoaster fiend and is on a mission to visit all the Six Flags amusement parks with her daughter. Every year, she travels for three weeks on a solo adventure to a new part of the world.

Follow on Social Media, she'd love to hear from you!

Website Email Newsletter

facebook.com/mhlebeaultauthor

x.com/mhlebeault

instagram.com/mhlebeault

amazon.com/author/mhlebeault

bookbub.com/authors/marie-helene-lebeault

goodreads.com/mhlebeault

linkedin.com/in/mhlebeault

tiktok.com/@mhlebeaultauthor

youtube.com/@mhlebeault

# ALSO BY THE AUTHOR

**The Chronicles of the Starborne Cadets**

Stars Beyond Realms

Shadows of Orion

Echoes of the Void

The Nebula's Heart

The Starborne Paradox

**Defenders of the Realm**

A Journey to Power

The Quest for the Emerald Rattleback

A Summer of Discovery

The Quest for the Sacred Tree

A Summer of Opposites

The Quest for the Phantom Feather

A Summer of Courage

The Quest for the Kraken's Ink

A Summer of Destiny

The Quest for the Cursed Mirrors

**The Evers Series**

The Ancestors' Key

The Academy

The Time Walker

The World Jumper

**Blood Magick Trilogy**

The Blood Mage

Blood Magick

Blood Legacy

## Standalones

Clarity Castle

What Happens Next?

Ghost Stories

Holiday Shifters

Echoes of Tomorrow

Utopia

## Picture Books

Fairy Grandmother: Millie Goes to Antarctica

Fairy Grandmother: Millie Goes to the North Pole

Fairy Grandmother: Millie Goes to China

Fairy Grandmother: Millie Goes to Africa

(Also available in French, Spanish, German, and Italian)

# CHAPTER
# ONE

PENELOPE LOOKED at herself in the mirror, making sure her red hair was all pulled back out of the way. She wasn't looking forward to this ceremony, though she knew it was necessary. The thing was, she would have rather skipped it and received her uniform in private.

It was the start of the second semester for her third year at the Institute. While the year had been going well so far, some things were still... sensitive.

"You are so beautiful!" Kaia gushed, clasping her hands together.

Penelope had elected to wear a simple gingham dress, the sort that you could work in. Kaia was wearing a full-out ballgown with her silver curls framing her round face perfectly.

"Thanks," Penelope murmured, blushing to match her hair. Being beautiful was never really high on her list of priorities, but Kaia was always so genuine about the compliment it made her feel beautiful. "You're gorgeous as usual. Did you get that dress for the royal ball you and Nolen went to over the Winter break?"

Kaia's fated mate, Nolen, was twin brother to Odele, who in turn was the fated mate of Adina. Adina was the youngest daughter of King Sydney and Queen Abigail, the two human monarchs of Eldavon.

Given Kaia's mother worked in the government, it was easy for her to be invited to royal balls.

Kaia swished back and forth. "It is. You don't think that it's too flashy, do you?"

Their other friend, Herja, stepped between them to view herself in the mirror. Her inky black hair was slicked back, and as usual she wore a simple all-black suit. Today, though, she had a pop of color in the form of a bright orange tie.

"It's not flashy," Herja said, straightening her tie. "You look like you, Kaia. All bright and shiny and wonderful."

It was Kaia's turn to blush.

Penelope stepped back, away from the other two. She was happy enough for her appearance, and this unwelcome stab of jealousy was making its opinion known.

The first semester had been good. Penelope was thriving in her studies this year and had even overtaken both Herja and Odele to be at the top of the class. Both Herja and Odele were pleased at having more competition, which was amusing to Penelope.

But Penelope still felt the absence of her fated mate.

She slipped from the dorm room where the three of them had been getting ready. The common room was filled with other students, ranging from year one to year five. None of them paid any attention to Penelope as she grabbed a random book off the bookshelf and headed out.

Right now, she just wanted to be alone.

Penelope was the first student in decades not to have a fated mate. Last year during the matching ceremony, she stood in front of everyone alone. And while she was still angry at times, sad at others, she had more or less figured out how to distract herself when these thoughts came up.

She had been talking with the school counselor twice a month since returning to the Institute after summer break, and that was helping—she was determined not to fall into the spirals of grief she had been trapped in when she first discovered she had no fated mate.

Footsteps sounded behind her, and when she turned, she found Kaia and Herja hurrying after her.

"I thought we were going together," Kaia said, frowning at her.

Penelope held up the book. "I just needed a little time alone."

Herja took the book. "Since when are you interested in geology?"

"I'm allowed to distract myself with anything I want," Penelope replied curtly, pulling the book away.

Herja opened her mouth, but Kaia elbowed her in the ribs.

"The ceremony's going to start soon, though, don't you think we should go to the dining hall?" Kaia asked. "I could put a muffling spell on your ears until it's time for it to start so you don't have to deal with the noise."

Penelope nodded once. "That'll be fine."

"I could use a muffling spell, too," Herja said as the three girls changed direction and started heading to the dining hall. "I've been overstimulated all day. I wish we didn't have to have this silly ceremony. Why does everyone have to watch while we're handed a bunch of clothes? Nobody enjoys watching it. It's so boring!"

Kaia drew her wand from the pouch she kept it in at her waist and pointed it at Penelope. "Block out the noises that will cause distress until the ceremony begins."

A warm feeling fluttered over Penelope's ears. It was like her head was wrapped up in cotton, only without the weight of it. She sighed as the sharpness to the surrounding sounds were relieved.

"Can you still hear us?" Herja asked.

Penelope nodded. "You don't cause me distress."

Herja stared stoically at her for a moment, then smiled. Kaia gave Herja the same spell and tension visibly melted off Herja's shoulders. She closed her eyes and sighed in relief.

"Where's Wickham?" Penelope asked, suddenly realizing that the fourth member of their little troupe was missing.

"He was helping Xena and Icarus." Kaia hummed. "Hey, have you ever thought about how similar the names of us third-years are? Herja, Vera, Xena, Lena, Jalene, Adina, Odele, Nolen, Kaia, Penelope, Wickham, Icarus. Not all of our names but quite a few. I'm always getting it confused."

Uh-oh, she was babbling. Penelope knew what that meant—Kaia had picked up on the reason for Penelope's melancholy. And now she was saying whatever popped into her head to distract from the fact that Penelope didn't have a mate.

"There are similarities, yeah," Herja said, her black brows arched over her silver eyes. She met Penelope's gaze and understanding dawned over her face. She winced.

Which only made Penelope feel worse.

"I don't need to be distracted by idle chatter," she said, but she smiled at Kaia. "Thanks for the effort, though."

Kaia gave her a weak smile in return. "Is there anything I can do to help?"

"I'm fine," Penelope said. "It's not like they're going to come to me and refuse to give me a uniform. Although I agree with Herja. I don't understand why there has to be so much pomp and circumstance around it all."

"I'm looking forward to the ceremony," Kaia said, then looked down at herself and laughed. "Or maybe I just like the excuse to dress up! We should do this more often."

Herja stuck her tongue out at Kaia. "Just put on your ballgowns for dinner, then."

"Maybe I will!"

Soon, they were in the dining hall. The vaulted ceilings glowed with chandeliers of light stones, lighting it all up bright as noon even though dusk had fallen long ago. The round tables had been pulled away from the front of the room, where a low stage was set up.

The three girls found an empty table to claim for themselves and their mates and settled down.

"I wish I knew how to make the spells that they use on our uniforms," Kaia said as she tucked her hands into her lap. "I would love to have all my clothes just be able to clean themselves and fix themselves and change as I change."

Penelope couldn't help but laugh at her. "But then you'd end up with far too many clothes and you wouldn't have an excuse to buy new dresses!"

"Hey, I love my dresses. I could wear a new one every day of the year, or change multiple times in the day," Kaia said, but she was smirking in how said she was joking about it.

"If I had clothes that had the spell, I'd only need one or two outfits," Herja said musingly, resting her chin in her hand. "That would be nice."

Penelope smiled. Her two friends were extremes with fashion. Kaia loved beautiful, fancy clothes. Anything that was hyper feminine was in her wheelhouse, and she was so unabashedly gleeful about her clothes it made Penelope feel more okay in exploring her own sense of style.

Herja, on the other hand, wore black. It made her look regal, that was certain. Penelope couldn't help but admire the poise she had in her simple clothing. Even the occasional pop of color seemed deliberate and gave her even more of a sense of confidence.

These uniforms would be helpful. Penelope didn't really enjoy spending too much time thinking about her clothes. They were all the same, so she would look like she fit in, even if she didn't entirely feel like it.

They were also magically spelled to stay intact when a dragon shifted between forms—which certainly prevented embarrassment as they learned how to make the change.

Wickham and Nolen joined them soon and the other third-year students gathered at nearby tables. They were all here... except Lena.

She had spent last summer at the Institute getting ahead on her schooling; her fated mate, a human named Victor, had spent the first semester here, and for this second semester they would spend time with his unit in the military.

Her absence was a stark reminder. If Lena hadn't ended up with a human, chances were that she and Penelope would have been matched... either that, or they both wouldn't have ended up with a mate. Penelope still wasn't entirely certain how all of this worked. The Stars decided which dragon-witch pair was perfectly matched.

Penelope shook her head quickly. No, she would not start into that spiral again. She was going to be present here and enjoy the ceremony.

Soon, the two headmasters took the stage. Headmaster Valiant, a witch, smiled out at them as he leaned against the podium. "Welcome back to the winter-spring semester. I hope you have all had a restful winter's break."

"Yeah!" one of the first-year students shouted.

Titters broke through the crowd, and Headmaster Valiant smiled at the student, who ducked their head.

"As most of you know by now, we will give our third-year students their uniforms tonight. Our professors have worked hard on preparing these uniforms; so without delay." He searched the crowd and smiled at the third-year students. "Please come up here and line up on the stage in a single line."

Penelope pushed her chair back, smoothing her hands on her dress.

This was the part that she was dreading most. First, the witches would be given uniforms to give to their dragon mates and then the dragons would get the witches' uniforms to hand them over. What had the teachers decided to do with her?

Adina and Odele were the first ones on the stage, holding hands and beaming at each other. Next came Nolen and Kaia, then Vera and Icarus, then Xena and Jalene, and finally Wickham and Herja.

Herja pressed a little closer to Jalene instead of Wickham and Penelope frowned. Things had seemed a little strained between the two of them in the first semester, but Penelope had assumed that was because Herja's studying habits had spilled out on all of them, and Wickham wanted more time to have his extracurricular studies in medicine.

Now she wondered if there was something else.

"When I call your name," Headmaster Valiant said, looking at the line of students, "you will come forward and accept your uniform from Headmaster Twila, then return to your seats."

Shock rippled through Penelope. This wasn't how it was supposed to be! For the past two years, it had been mates presenting their uniforms to each other. So why—

Oh.

So that was how the professors dealt with her being mateless. Her cheeks flushed. If this was supposed to stop Penelope's lack of a mate from being highlighted, it failed. Her shoulders slumped forward, and she wished the ground would open up and swallow her whole.

Not only didn't she have a mate, but now the others were losing out on tradition because of it. That wasn't fair.

She breathed in deep and waited for her name to be called. This would be over soon. She just had to hang on until it was.

# CHAPTER
# TWO

WICKHAM KNOTTED his long silver hair around the hair tie he was using to keep it out of his face during the rest of the break.

They were departing from the normal curriculum and including the witch's self-defense training this year. While the tensions between Eldavon and the neighboring kingdom of Odentia weren't as intense as they had been, it was decided that the witches needed to know more physical means of defending themselves instead of relying on magic.

Professor Delphine, the dragon professor for the third-year students, clapped her hands lightly. "Line up with your mates now, students," she called. "We will practice our thought-to-though communication."

"You'll practice with me," the witch professor, Gable, told Penelope. "It is important for all witches and all dragons to communicate with one another, not just with their mates."

Wickham noted Penelope's half-hidden flinch, but her expression didn't change as she nodded.

He raised his hand. "Can we have another few minutes? The physical exertion took a lot out of me."

He had gotten sick over the Winter break. Mother and Father both said it was because he was working too hard, although he didn't think it was. He'd ended up in bed with a nasty cough for two weeks and while he was mostly better now, he still found himself wiped out a bit too easily.

"Mind-to-mind speak isn't physically difficult," Professor Gable said. "Find a comfortable place to sit with your mate."

The students broke off into pairs. Wickham eyed Penelope one last time before he turned, too. There wasn't anything he could do to help her and Professor Gable was practicing with her. He needed to concentrate on his own issues here.

Namely, that things were still awkward with Herja.

When they had found out they were fated mates, he had been thrilled... but quickly found out that Herja didn't share his joy. Since then, he had been determined not to let his hopes of having a romantic relationship with his mate not ruin his friendship with her.

After all, Herja was his best friend, and she was too important for him to make mistakes with.

It was difficult because every time he made her laugh, butterflies erupted in his stomach. But he was determined, and he would not let himself mess this up.

Herja wanted nothing like that. And who said that mates had to be romantic anyway? There were plenty of dragon-witch pairs who didn't fall in love.

The two of them sat down in a corner, facing each other. Herja's lips were pinched together tightly, like she was upset. Wickham sighed. What was she upset about? Was it him or something else.

"To begin, look into your mate's eyes," Professor Delphine instructed.

Wickham did so and Herja twitched in discomfort.

"Now, I want you both to concentrate on the image of an apple. Picture it in your minds."

Wickham tried—but almost immediately, his mind turned to the apple trees that grew outside the new house that his family had just moved into. It was a bigger home this time, so that the twins could each have their own room.

And thinking of the twins made him think they had just celebrated their thirteenth birthday. Which meant that this summer, they would make the trip to the Silver Springs. They would be revealed as either dragon, witch, or human. Both of them were talking about being witches like him. But that wasn't how it worked, and he didn't want them to be disappointed.

Worse, if one of them was a witch and the other wasn't, it might make them jealous. He didn't want his brothers to develop a rift between them.

"That's not an apple, I can see it on your face," Herja said, her eyes narrowed.

Wickham rubbed his forehead. Everyone else was still staring into each other's eyes in the quiet classroom. "Sorry," he whispered. "I'm just out of it today."

Supposedly, Odentia was going to make another attempt to kidnap the children this year. If they did, his brothers would be in danger.

Wickham knew he shouldn't listen to rumors. It had been the same rumor every year since Odentia tried to kidnap the third-year students on their trip, three years ago. Those years, though, his brothers weren't in the group who would go up.

Not that he thought Odentia would target his family directly... just that the rumors hit closer to home right now.

"Wick," Herja hissed.

He shook his head and looked back at her. They gazed into each other's eyes and Herja twitched again.

Wickham looked away. It was too uncomfortable to maintain eye contact like that when she clearly didn't want it. He covered his eyes with his hands, letting everything go black. The sound of breathing surrounded him.

"Okay, let's try this again," Wickham said, hoping that their talking wasn't distracting the other students too much.

He lowered his hands again and met her gaze. Normally Herja didn't have this much trouble maintaining eye contact; at least, he'd never noticed her handing difficulties before. Maybe there was something different about the intensity of this moment?

Wickham knew that was the case for himself. Even though they were surrounded by others, something about being told to stare into each other's eyes made it all the more intimate.

*Apple,* he thought.

He imagined the fruit, plump and green-gold. Those were his favorites. He imagined the contradictory sweet and tart flavor of its juice, then thought of the apple pies Mother made. Apple pie, apple-sauce, apple crumble. They tasted like love.

He turned his brain back to the actual fruit, imaging it. The image seemed to grow sharper in his mind, the gold-green skin taking on a reddish hue. His heart leapt—they were doing it! They were sharing the mental image of their apples!

But even as he thought this, the image fizzled out entirely.

Herja threw her hands into the air. "Wickham!"

He jumped, blinking rapidly. "What?"

"We almost had it. You need to concentrate on what's going on here instead of thinking about other things." Herja got to her feet and stomped them.

At first, Wickham thought she was even angrier than he realized. Then he felt the prickling in his own feet and quickly got to his feet, too, stomping them to get rid of the pins and needles sensation of his feet falling asleep.

"How long was that?" he grumbled. It only felt like a few seconds.

Herja rubbed her temples. "I don't know. But we were almost there. Then you started to think about apple pies and I lost you."

"That's not what happened," Wickham protested. "I thought about the apple pie first, before we connected."

"You did not!"

Professor Delphine came over to them. "Lower your voices. This is not a time to fight; if I understand correctly, you could briefly share the image?"

Herja scowled. "Then Wickham thought about apple pies."

"I thought about them first," Wickham insisted.

"You did not—"

"Herja." Professor Delphine frowned at her. "Don't start arguing. I'm surprised that you haven't read up on this. It's a good sign that you two could connect at all, and clearly you got an after-shock thought. That's a good sign, too."

Herja pushed her short black hair out of her face. "But we were supposed to be—"

"Herja. Please stay after class so we can talk," Professor Delphine said, her tone strict.

Wickham rubbed his hands on his trousers, then folded his arms. It felt like only a few seconds that he and Herja had been concentrating on each other, but the rest of the class was up and moving again. Nolen and Kaia were laughing together and Wickham had a surge of jealousy.

Clearly, they were already speaking mind-to-mind.

Why did he have such a hard time connecting with Herja when they had already been friends before they became mates? Meanwhile, the others seemed to be just so perfectly connected. Kaia and Nolen especially were just so perfect with each other.

That was what he wanted. He wanted this to be easy... was this his fault? Was he putting too much pressure on Herja, even though he had promised himself he wouldn't?

Or maybe he was really just distracted.

He moved to the side of the classroom, where their drinks and snacks were. Herja continued to move through various stretches while Wickham nibbled at a few snacks.

Herja really could have approached it a little nicer, though. She didn't immediately have to accuse him of messing it up. And she outright said he was lying about thinking about apple pie first! He thought she knew him better than that—why would he lie about something so stupid?

"Hey." Penelope grabbed a handful of crackers. "Herja giving you a hard time, huh?"

Wickham shrugged, not really wanting to get into it. "I think we're both tired and stressed is all."

He couldn't compare his relationship with Herja to Nolen and Kaia's. For one thing, he wasn't like either of them and neither was Herja. They just had to learn how to go at their own pace... and besides that, it wasn't as though Herja really opened up even without adding the telepathic link to it.

"We have to be patient," he said aloud. "And I have to remember that Herja doesn't think the same way I do, and so I need to be more understanding."

Penelope munched on the crackers, her expression blank. "Like Kaia said, communication. She and Nolen only are as in tune with each other as they are because they learned how to talk to each other better over the summer."

Wickham winced. "Is it obvious I was being jealous of them?"

"Everyone's jealous of them. Well, maybe not Odele and Adina." Penelope glanced at those two, who were currently mimicking each other's movements.

Penelope was doing well with being the only one without a mate. She was always so confident and in control... Wickham wished he could mimic that confidence better.

"I'm gonna get back at it," she said abruptly, heading over to where Professor Gable was quietly instructing Vera and Icarus.

Wickham washed down his last bites of food with a glass of water, then stretched out his back. He headed back to Herja, who now had her fingertips pressed to her temples. Pain was etched on her face and Wickham hurried over.

"Are you okay?"

Herja straightened. "I'll be fine. It's nothing unusual. I'm tired, though. I asked Professor Delphine for the rest of class off—you can practice with Pen."

Wickham still followed Herja as she gathered her things. "Are you sure? Did I do something wrong?"

Herja shook her head. "No. I'm just not in the right frame of mind for this today. I'm sorry for yelling at you—this is me, not you. I just need some time alone, okay?"

Wickham handed her bag to her. "Is there anything I can do?"

"No. I need time alone."

Wickham wanted to ask again but bit his tongue. He wanted to help her, and his instinct was to find the thing he could fix and then fix it. However, as the herbalist back home, Kassandra, liked to say, sometimes the best thing for a patient was patience.

He nodded once. "I hope you feel better soon."

"Thanks," Herja muttered as she left the classroom.

He watched her go, wishing he really could read her mind. Was she really upset with him or was it something else like she claimed now? Had she caught something else in his thoughts when they were trying to connect?

Oh no... did she realize he was fighting this crush he had on her?

Fighting the urge to run after her, Wickham turned back into the classroom. Herja said she needed space. He needed to give her space. They'd talk when Herja was ready, not before.

# CHAPTER
# THREE

NORMALLY, you couldn't pay Herja to miss class. Even now, it scraped painfully at the back of her mind that she really ought to be in class.

She wasn't getting anything out of it, though, not when she was so distracted by all this... stuff. And even worse, she blew up at Wickham for no reason! Just another thing for her to feel bad about. Even though she had apologized, it didn't feel like enough. She was going to have to do more.

Right now, though, she was lying in bed with a hot water bottle tucked up against her back. Of course she'd be dealing with cramps on top of everything else.

"Unclear," she read, going over the first paper and then the second one again. "What's the point of all those doctor's appointments if I'm not going to get a clear answer?"

She tucked the papers together and set them on her nightstand, then lay on her stomach and adjusted the hot water bottle onto her back again. The cramps were bad now only because it was a combined pain; all the dragons were getting ready to change their forms and until they were able to completely change, they'd remain having muscle cramps.

They'd be better soon enough. Just a couple more days and it'd go back to normal.

The door opened and Herja groaned, realizing she had forgotten to close the curtains that would dampen the sounds between her bed and the others.

"Herja?" Kaia's voice came in. "You awake?"

She groaned again, but Kaia had a knack of making her feel better. "Come on in. Did you bring chocolate?"

Kaia laughed as she brushed aside the curtain and sat on the edge of the bed. "Wick was worried about you. You want to talk?"

Herja sighed. "If you don't mind me rambling."

Her heart constricted. She should have talked to Wickham about this... that was why they were mates, wasn't it? So they could talk about these things?

"I don't mind," Kaia said.

Herja rolled back to her side, holding the hot water bottle in place. "I got the results from my last test back. It's unclear if I have autism. More testing is required. I'm so tired of having to talk with all these professionals and it takes forever! When I decided I wanted to get a proper diagnosis, I thought it would be easy. Either I'm neurotypical or neurodivergent. Not this weird middle-ground limbo."

Kaia nodded sympathetically. "We don't really have the resources we need for it, do we? But I guess it really is that our understanding of the mind keeps evolving, especially as society changes. So... with any luck, your difficulties will make it easier for the next generation?"

"Hopefully."

She hadn't thought about it like that before, though. It made Herja feel better to think that she could be part of the learning process for the entire kingdom. Eldavon paid more attention to their social structure than other kingdoms—although several other kingdoms were following suit—but that didn't mean it was perfect.

Perfection didn't exist. Something that annoyed Herja to no end. She just wished that perfection could be real.

Herja rolled to a sitting position and pulled the hot water bottle to her stomach. "I guess I can't complain too much. Professor Farrow is putting in a lot of effort to help me. I will not give up; I'll figure it out, eventually."

Kaia tilted her head, her warm eyes shrewd. "Have you told Wickham about it yet?"

"No."

"Why?"

"I don't want to burden him."

Kaia let out an exasperated sigh. "Herja, you know Wick better than that! If you had nothing wrong at all, you'd have to make something up so Wickham could help you with something. The boy cannot sit still, he always wants to be doing something. You're burdening him more by not sharing."

Herja couldn't help but laugh about that. It kind of was true. Wickham certainly was the type who wanted to help others to a fault.

Her brevity didn't last long, however. She scooted back and leaned against the headrest of her bed. "I guess maybe I don't want to tell him right now because he'll try to fix it, and there's nothing to be fixed. Like when I told him all this... stuff about not being adopted."

She waved at her nightstand. She kept the records from her time at the orphanage there. Apparently, all these years of feeling worthless because nobody wanted to adopt her wasn't true... she was the one who didn't want to be adopted.

Between running away from foster homes to throwing temper tantrums when meeting new people, she had made herself unadoptable.

There had been families who wanted to adopt her. She rejected them so often that the caretakers at the orphanage had removed her from the adoptable listings. Every year, she had loudly proclaimed how much she didn't want to be adopted when in the truth; she did. So. That was something to get used to.

"Do you know when the next specialist will show up?" Kaia asked.

"No idea. But it'll happen when it happens."

Kaia patted her shoulder. "If you have anything else that you need to talk about, just let me know, okay?"

Herja nodded slowly. "I was just thinking about my records, and how I self-sabotaged myself so much growing up. I understand it now, but there isn't much I can do about the past, is there?"

"No. But you can figure out how to change as you move forward," Kaia suggested.

"Hmm." That was true, but it was still something Herja hadn't quite figured out just yet.

She still wanted to be adopted. She wanted to have a family. Becoming close to her friends here at the Institute had shown her she wasn't better off alone, like she had convinced herself. Community was important. Connection was important.

The thing was, though, she didn't know how to integrate herself into the community or make connections. When she tried to do it on purpose, she only ended up failing.

"You won't tell Wick, right?" Herja said, twisting her sleeve up between her fingers.

"Of course not. Not unless you want me to tell him."

"Well... well, I want to be adopted. But I'm pretty sure I'm too old and I have too much of an attitude problem," Herja admitted quietly. It was the first time she had said it out loud. "Besides, I'm sixteen. In two more years, I'll be a legal adult. What's the point of being adopted for only two years?"

"You can have a family after you're eighteen, too," Kaia said.

Herja shrugged. Now that she had brought it up, she didn't actually want to continue the conversation. It was just... so personal. While she had started being more open with her friends, some walls still felt necessary.

"It'd just be going through the motions," Herja said quickly, waving her hand. "I'm fine."

"You could talk to Mr. Bryce about it, or Professor Farrow."

Herja shook her head, abruptly done with this topic—more than done, in fact. She let out a huff of breath. "Maybe. But I don't want to talk about this anymore. How did you and Nolen end up telepathically talking so easily?"

Kaia pulled back slightly, blinking a few times.

"I saw the way you two were, you were already talking mind-to-mind. I read that it's the hardest part of the mate-bond and that normally a full conversation between mates can't happen until after a dragon changes so—"

"Stop." Kaia held up her hands. "Give me a minute to catch up."

Herja bit her lips together.

"Okay. So you don't want to talk about your adoption records. Instead, you want to talk about Nolen and me... is that because you want help figuring out how you and Wickham can work better together or because you're asking me how things are going with Nolen?"

"Er..."

Kaia arched a silver brow. "It's okay if you just want help for you and Wickham. I've been feeling the tension between you."

Herja groaned and flopped over, burying her face into her pillows. "It's that obvious?"

"Yeah."

"You and Nolen are just so smooth together. Even when you fight, you don't really fight. And your summer together seems like it was so idyllic!"

Kaia burst out laughing. "Herja! How can you hear I overwhelmed him with my family, and he didn't talk to me about what he was feeling and think it was idyllic? It wasn't. We just figured out how to talk to each other."

"I don't know how to talk to Wickham."

"Yes, you do. You've been talking to him for two years."

Herja shrugged. "Maybe we're just not compatible as mates."

"Why not?"

"Because I can't talk to him!"

Kaia held her hands into the air. "Okay, okay. I guess you're not really in the mood to talk about it."

"We have made no progress in the projects that the two of us are assigned," Herja continued, hating the tears forming in her eyes. "You saw today—"

"No, I was a bit too busy."

"It wasn't good. I messed up and broke our connection and then I blamed him."

Kaia sighed. "Maybe today just wasn't the right day to do it, then? I think you've got a lot on your mind... maybe you should talk with the professors to get a few days out of class, if it will help."

Herja nodded slowly. She hated the idea of taking time off her classes but if she was going to blow up like this all the time...

"And as for you and Wickham," she continued, her voice growing firmer, "you need to just talk to him. Stop putting so much pressure on yourself."

"What do you mean by that?"

Kaia gave her a pointed look, causing Herja to blush. Oh, she knew alright. Ever since elementary school she had been forcing herself to learn more and keep going harder than everyone else.

She had done her best to be at least one grade ahead of her peers. Now she wasn't entirely certain why it was so important. It hadn't pushed her any closer to her goals... and when she had decided she wanted to be a queen one day; she had also decided to push harder than ever.

Only, now she wasn't sure if she wanted to be queen. There was so much involved in that; she couldn't just make plans to improve people's lives, she had to be aware of the various ways people would be affected. She had to know how to understand people... and she wasn't entirely certain that was something she could do.

"Take time for self-care," Kaia said. "You must allow yourself time to rest and heal and have fun. Like working on your book."

Herja blushed deeper. The book she had started at the beginning of the last school year was currently taking up three notebooks and wasn't finished yet. So far, Kaia was the only one she shared it with, her reasoning that if anyone could be encouraging about it, Kaia would be.

"I still take time to write," she mumbled. "Just not as much as I did over the summer break."

"As long as you're taking the time to yourself and not get burnt out," Kaia advised wisely. She smiled. "So, you want me to get you some chocolate?"

"Yes, please."

Kaia nodded once. "Be right back."

As she left, Herja adjusted the hot water bottle again. Burnt out. Maybe that was her problem. Maybe she had run out of steam at sixteen years old. It was something to think about.

In the meantime, rather than pondering everything that was going wrong, Herja closed her eyes and started to daydream about her story. Kaia was right. Thinking about that was much more pleasant than continual angst over her problems.

# CHAPTER
# FOUR

KAIA LAZILY PADDLED her feet through the water, enjoying the warmth of it. Rain pounded on the windows but inside the large room, the temperature was magically controlled, as was the water. It was beautifully relaxing after a long, sweaty day of training.

Wickham rested nearby, looking despondent while Penelope ducked under the water and resurfaced.

"You want to talk?" Kaia asked Wickham.

After her summer blunders with Nolen, she was trying to be more aware of when other people might want to talk, rather than simply trying to make them not feel the negative thing. Distraction was all well and good, but sometimes things had to be discussed to be fixed.

"I'm just worried about Herja," Wickham admitted.

"She'd going through a lot of personal stuff right now."

"I know, I just feel like I need to be supporting her, but she won't let me. I feel like she's shutting me out." He frowned as he fixed his long, silver hair back atop his head to keep it from getting wet.

Penelope joined them. "You should mix some painkillers for her. The cramps of our dragon forms are bad enough, but period cramps make it even worse."

Wickham nodded once. "I'll do that. There are some special herbs that always work with my mother, maybe they'll help Herja, too."

"It's weird that we've all synched up, isn't it?" Penelope asked. "It's nice to have the warning though—Herja's always comes in first."

Wickham's brow furrowed, and he gave her a strange look.

"Are you comfortable talking about this?" Kaia asked. "Talking about periods, I mean?"

She knew that not all people were as open with talking about periods as Penelope's family. It wasn't exactly a taboo subject in her own family but she was surprised at how casually Penelope would bring it up.

"Oh, yeah. It's fine." Wickham waved a hand.

Penelope frowned at Kaia. "Why wouldn't it be?"

"Well, for one thing he's a boy," Kaia responded. "For another, his little sister is still so young, it wouldn't have come up around anymore."

"I still have a mother, though. And I've been working with various medical professionals for three years now," Wickham said. "I'm learning to be a doctor, I can't be squeamish about normal bodily functions."

Kaia hummed. "Guess so."

Penelope nodded once. "And as far as Herja's issues go, she'll talk when she's ready to talk... although knowing Herja, she might not. She doesn't like to admit she's not one-hundred percent, does she?"

"She doesn't," Wickham agreed. "And that's what worries me. I'm supposed to be her support and help, but how can I do that without her talking to me? I can't even tell if it's me she doesn't trust or if it's something else entirely. And," he added slowly, "I feel guilty talking about her at all without her knowing about it."

Kaia hummed as she nodded slowly. "I understand that. You're probably right, Herja is a private person. She wouldn't want us to be discussing her like this."

Penelope grimaced. "Yeah, you're right. So! Change of subject. Kaia, I saw you got a letter from home. Anything you want to share?"

This elicited a flinch.

Unfortunately, her flinch got exactly the reaction that Kaia was hoping to avoid. Both of her friends' faces fell into concern, and even when Kaia waved her hand, as though it was nothing, their concern remained.

"It's really not important," she said, trying to appear casual.

"And we know that's not true," Wickham said, pulling himself out of the water. He sat on the side of the pool next to her and nudged her with his shoulder. "What's going on?"

Kaia sighed. Even though she didn't feel like she really should share about it—after all, she wasn't certain it was something worth the worry it would evoke—she also kind of felt like she wanted to. The big thing was that she didn't want her friends to end up worried about her when she wasn't all thatworried about herself.

Not anymore, at least.

"Mother wrote me because Finnegan escaped the prison he was being held in. Nobody got hurt," she added quickly, seeing the worry in her friends' eyes. "But she thought I should know, since I was so afraid last year."

If she was honest, she wasn't entirely certain why she wasn't more afraid right now. She should be terrified! After all, Finnegan haunted her nightmares for a full year before she finally confronted him again.

Maybe it was because she had learned more techniques to help with her anxiety since then. She had come to recognize the tightness between her shoulders and the distraction in her mind before things got really bad, and was able to calm herself.

If that didn't work, she had her magical potions that would physically calm her body, allowing her to get out of the fight-or-flight response that she'd grown used to being in. Kaia didn't particularly like taking medications, but sometimes she had to. It didn't do her any good to sit and wallow in panic when there was something that could bring her out of it.

"Are you alright?" Wickham asked her worriedly.

"I think so," Kaia replied with a curt nod. "I'm done with being afraid all the time and when I saw him last year, he wasn't so terrifying. We know how to defend ourselves better, so I don't have to worry so much about me or anyone else."

Penelope frowned at her, like she didn't believe it.

"Besides," Kaia said with a bright smile, "Finnegan doesn't have the resources to come after me and even if he did, why would he? I'm not exactly important to him."

"But you were the one who got him transferred from the Odentia prison to Eldavon," Wickham said. "Do you think he'll be angry for you getting him taken away from his home kingdom?"

"No."

Penelope squeezed water out of her long red braid. "I'd agree on that one—I've been writing with Victor and Lena. They were part of the group that went to Odentia to help with the famine relief. Apparently Odentia prisons are horrible. They're not even treated like people, let alone given help for their problems."

Kaia nodded, her chin tucked against her chest as she watched the eddies of water. She had heard more about what prisons over in Odentia were like, and it honestly horrified her. If she hadn't understood how someone could try to kidnap or hurt children, after hearing about Odentia's punishments, she understood it now.

Secretly, though, she wondered if it really was her fault. She was the one who had Finnegan brought over. No, she wasn't responsible for keeping him locked away, nor was she the one who let him escape. But he was in Eldavon because she worked with the two kings and two queens to make it happen.

If anyone got hurt because of him, would it be on her head?

"Kaia?" Penelope splashed her knee.

Kaia shook her head, trying to get those thoughts out. "I don't think I want to talk about this anymore. Finnegan has no logical reason to come after me, especially not when we're so protected. More likely, he'll be going after the Silver Springs, what with his obsession with magic."

Wickham and Penelope glanced at each other.

"What?"

"Welllll...." Penelope pulled out the word like she was searching for the right ones to come after it. "You said you don't want to talk about it, then brought up another point that is kinda worth talking about."

Kaia groaned as she kicked the water. "Maybe what I need to do is go see the school counselor."

Wickham bumped her shoulder again. "You're probably right, though. I bet he gets caught trying to get to the Silver Springs. Unless he goes after the rumor of the new springs."

"New springs?" Kaia asked, her eyes widening. She hadn't heard anything about a potential new source of magic! "What are you talking about?"

"Yeah," Penelope echoed. "What are you talking about?"

"There's a rumor going around that a second magical springs has been found," Wickham said. "Where children who were... well, they're saying 'rejected' by the Silver Springs have a second chance to gain magic."

Kaia's jaw dropped. "Rejected? But humans have magic! Just look at the kings and queens. If we didn't have a human king and queen along with the witch and dragon, Eldavon would fail!"

"Humans have Earth Magic," Penelope said, her fiery eyebrows drew together. "Where is this rumor even coming from?"

Wickham shrugged. "There were a handful of workers from across the sea who were talking about it over the summer."

"That's that, then," Penelope said as she pulled herself out of the water and grabbed a hand towel. "They don't know what they're talking about."

Kaia wasn't so sure, though. After all, the Silver Springs were only one magic source. It was said in the old days there were dragons and witches that spread all over the globe, and now only Eldavon had them.

"There's no other type of magic besides Sun, Moon, and Earth, anyway," Penelope continued. "So it has to be fake. You can't just change the type of magic you are."

"What about the stars?" Kaia asked absently. After all, the Stars were important, too, and yet they had given no one magic directly as far as she knew. They could have started to give another gift.

Penelope frowned. "If it was the stars, why wouldn't they just use the Silver Springs? Where are these 'backups' supposed to be, anyway?"

Wickham shook his head. "Somewhere in the mountains, I guess."

"There. It's fake. How would people across the sea know about this before we in Eldavon knew about it?" Penelope demanded. She wrapped her towel around her waist, water still dripping from her swimsuit. "It's all fake rumors. Odentia must be causing trouble again. There isn't any other type of magic."

"I'm not so sure," Wickham said. "The Chameleon Sprites have their own magic. So does the Emerald Rattleback and other—"

"I don't want to talk about rumors," Penelope said flatly.

Kaia was surprised to hear her be so defensive about this. Pen wasn't the sort of person to just shut down the possibilities of different things. Was there something about a possible new source of magic that was bothering her?

"Do you want to race?" Penelope asked.

Oh, that was definitely a deliberate attempt to distract them and herself. Kaia's brows furrowed in worry. If she had known it would end up here, she never would have brought any of it up. But how could she know where it would end up? Besides, she wasn't the one who brought up the letter in the first place.

"Pen," she said, then stopped. It was clear Penelope didn't want to talk about any of this. It wouldn't do any good to keep pushing. "I hurt my ankle while training today and Professor Gable told me to avoid straining it. Maybe we can race down the pool using only our hands?"

Penelope looked down at herself, clearly weighing the benefits of having to dry off a second time.

"Wait," Wickham said as he held up his hands. "We're not finished this discussion."

"No, we are," Penelope said.

"But—"

Kaia nudged him. "I'd like to be done with it, too. Maybe we can talk again later?"

Wickham lowered his hands, looking a bit perturbed. Kaia gave him an apologetic smile, then leapt off the edge of the pool. She started paddling with her hands, trying her best to keep her legs dragging behind her.

Soon, the sounds of splashing behind her caught up and then surpassed her as Penelope joined into the pool.

But even with the physical exertion, Kaia couldn't help but keep thinking. It seemed to her that there was something happening in Eldavon. And she just wasn't sure what that something would turn out to be.

# CHAPTER
# FIVE

HERJA LOOKED at the swirling black clouds above the camp. Blue and yellow lightning flickered in the darkness, and she could hear the distant punch of thunder.

"I hope it stays up there," she murmured, rubbing her sweaty palms against her legs.

After a long trek using handcarts to pack their things, rather than the wagons from last year, they were finally at the Storm Mountains. They would camp in the valley beneath Thunder Ridge. Though the campsite was used every year, there were no permanent structures here.

Since the dragons were learning how to shift to their dragon forms and fight to protect the witches that way, they were learning how to work with limited supplies. Foraging and taking care of themselves and learning how to work together. And of course, the flying.

The flying. Herja wasn't entirely certain she wanted to do that— here, at least. Rocs lived in those thundering peaks and even if they didn't, the mountains had a constant swirl of storm above them. Hence their name, Storm Mountains and Thunder Ridge.

Yeah. This was a great place to be.

Unfortunately, a roc feather was vital to the next stage of the witches' journeys. They needed it for the special quill that they'd make for their spell books. It would keep track of their spells in a special ink, which they would make next year.

"Herja, can you grab that rope?"

She turned to where Wickham was struggling to set up a tent. Quickly, she hurried over and helped him. This year, the students would all have their own tent rather than sharing. The two professors had their tents in the middle of the campsite and girls would be on one side with boys on the other.

"The Storm Mountains are known for their unpredictable weather patterns," she told him as she helped tug the rope taut. Wickham wrapped his end around one stake. "They have a penchant for sudden rainfall and thunderstorms and strong winds."

Wickham checked to make sure the stake was secure before he rocked back on his heels. "Professor Gable says that the steep cliffs and rocky valley on this side offers protection from the storms and rocs. They don't like to come over this way and the rain doesn't collect, it runs off."

"Professor Delphine said that, too," Herja said, glancing up at the storm clouds again nervously.

The witches and dragons both had erected sturdy tents and shelters for sleeping, cooking, and times to just hang out together. There was a strict policy of no tent-visits, it didn't matter who was visiting who.

"Now that we're all set up, do you want to go explore a bit?" Wickham asked.

Herja dropped her gaze from the storm clouds. "Uuuhhhh... well I think it should be fine. But let me bring my earmuffs."

She jogged back to her tent and grabbed the earmuffs that Wickham had charmed to help muffle distant rumbles. They were awfully hot, as the Storm Mountains were already well out of winter and into spring. Wickham was still working on making them cooler, so Herja could wear them for longer bouts of time.

For right now, though, keeping that rumble at bay would help her feel better.

She and Wickham informed the professors they would be going

into the forest and headed out. After their experiences with the Silent Marshes and the Golden Forest, it was simple enough to navigate this forest. The trees were thin and the brush low, so they could see a good distance around themselves.

Furthermore, if they did get lost all they would have to do was go down the mountain and they'd eventually come to the valley. The valley itself was so bare that you could see camp no matter where you started from.

"We'll be starting to try to shift to dragon form tomorrow," Herja said as she and Wickham trekked upward. "I've read all about it. It's a strong internal magic that a dragon has to channel in order to get the dragon form to come out. I feel the heat of the fires in my chest and stomach sometimes. That's a good sign. I should be able to make the transformation..."

Her voice trailed off doubtfully. Truth was, she had attempted to make the transformation before. She had even gotten Professor Farrow to try to help her. So far, she hadn't been able to do something as simple as grow a single scale.

It was something you had to feel out, apparently. No amount of reading and studying would help with that.

"It will come with time," Wickham said. He reached for her hand and suddenly pulled back, clearing his throat as he did so.

Herja frowned at him. "You've been acting weird all year."

"Have I?"

"You have." Herja winced at her accusatory tone. "Er... sorry. I didn't mean for it to sound like I'm starting a fight. It's just that you're not acting like yourself and I'm a bit worried."

Wickham shrugged. "I guess it's just that things are weird right now. I've got a lot on my mind and I don't know what to say or do to help you. I know that waiting for the tests and results is rubbing your nerves raw and I can't really do anything about that."

Herja fell silent. She wasn't aware that she was acting 'raw' around her friends—in fact, she had thought she was doing a pretty good job at acting normally.

"I said something wrong, didn't I?" Wickham asked.

"No. You were just being honest. That isn't wrong." Herja pushed her short hair from her face. "But how can you tell?"

"You tensed up. You started to look at the ground when usually you look up at the path ahead or at the sky," Wickham replied. He came to a stop and turned to Herja; his warm eyes pinched at the corners with concern. "Do you want to talk about things, or do you want distractions?"

Herja shook her head, a lump rising in her throat. Normally she'd just shrug off the question, but the way Wickham looked at her was just so obviously genuine. She could see that he was hurting from her hurt. It made her feel... guilty.

There wasn't anything she could do about her own feelings, but the least she should try was not to hurt her friends with it!

"Distractions," she finally managed to say around the lump in her throat. "That will be best."

Because then at least Wickham wouldn't continue to be hurt by it.

---

KAIA PRESSED both of her hands to her mouth to remind herself that she wasn't allowed to speak out loud. Nolen was navigating a simple obstacle course, blindfolded. It was a test for their telepathic communication. No longer looking into each other's eyes and focusing on the same thing, instead she was on the sidelines, and he was the one navigating the course.

Tomorrow, it would be the other way around for a brand-new course that the teachers put together.

Nolen stumbled on a small rock Kaia hadn't noticed and she focused again, staring intently at the path Nolen had to follow until he got to the ladder. He stood still a minute, then bent as though getting to his hands and knees.

*No, no, no! There's a ladder next.* Kaia pushed the thoughts toward him.

Nolen froze up, half crouched. He shook his head as though trying to clear something muffled from his head. Kaia felt herself tense and when she tried to push even harder, the thread that held them together snapped. She dropped her hands and closed her eyes, breathing deeply.

They had limited time of Nolen standing still before Professor Delphine called an end to their attempt. She had to clear her thoughts —putting too much pressure on herself and Nolen only ever backfired.

She released her breath and opened her eyes again. Reaching back out, she found that thread that shimmered in her mind like the star threads that bound them together. She sent a thought along it and Nolen carefully stepped forward.

*That's it. Two more steps and there's a ladder.*

He stepped forward twice—and ran into the ladder. Kaia flinched as the class tittered, but Nolen quickly recovered himself. He climbed to the top, and Kaia tried to visualize the beam he would then have to cross. But he didn't move.

What was the matter? Kaia frowned, leaning in as she tried again.

Nolen felt along with his hands, sliding forward cautiously.

Kaia got the feeling something was wrong just before he suddenly pitched to the side. He fell, landing in the net with a grunt. She rushed forward to make sure he was okay, and only when she was under the beam did she see it—it wasn't flat on the top, but sharply sloped to one side.

If she had been receiving his feedback as much as she should have been, she'd have known. She let out a sigh of frustration and Nolen pulled his blindfold off.

"Well done," Professor Delphine called, clapping her hands. "You two made it the farthest today."

Kaia offered a hand to Nolen and helped him out of the net. Frustration budded in her gut. Neither of them had seen how the other students did, and she had to admit that she hated having the audience. Each couple took their turn being first and last.

Except Penelope. She was randomly paired with witches or worked with Professor Gable. She was pretty good at connecting telepathically to everyone, but Kaia could see the increased despondence in her after these trials.

Suddenly, her frustration turned to guilt. Her fingers twined through Nolen's. Why should she be frustrated at the progress she and her mate were making when they were at the top of the class? It wasn't fair to either of them, or their classmates. And, she had a mate. She could make steady progress without wondering what each day would look like.

"Well done, both of you," Professor Delphine praised as she smiled at them.

Kaia nodded.

"The rest of you," Professor Delphine said as she turned to the other students. "You have all done wonderfully. You may not feel like your progress is as good as it ought to be, but you have all progressed faster than any other class I've taught. You're all free for lunch."

Kaia sighed. Her stomach was rumbling —food was a good idea.

"After lunch, the witches will go with Professor Gable and work on their spell work while the dragons will join me. We'll scale some small cliffs and practice changing forms."

Nolen's hand tightened on Kaia's. His normally stoic expression faltered. "We aren't expected to fly, are we?"

"No. It's a practice to get used to being at an elevated height."

Herja's hand shot into the air. "What about the rocs and thunder?"

"Rocs don't come out during the day unless there's a severe storm, and while yes, the weather patterns can be somewhat unpredictable, there are warning signs. So long as we have blue skies, there is nothing to worry about."

"But what about the thunder?"

Professor Delphine ignored her as she clapped her hands. "That's all for now, students. Lunch time. Reconvene in an hour and a half."

"Let's go," Nolen said as he tugged Kaia's hand. "I'm starved."

Kaia nodded. She kept an eye on Penelope as they walked away. Everyone naturally drifted to their fated mate. Her heart ached. How isolating must this be for her friend? But was there anything she could do about it?

# CHAPTER
# SIX

HERJA TORE INTO HER SANDWICH. She had slept in this morning, meaning she'd ended up missing breakfast. Wickham had offered her snacks continuously, but she'd been too stubborn to accept them.

Normally she disliked egg salad, but this was the best egg salad sandwich she had ever had! She leaned back against a large rock as she chewed. Her meal was already half-gone, and she still felt like she hadn't eaten a thing.

"How far did you get?" Kaia asked Penelope. The others were still setting out their lunches.

Penelope shrugged. "I got to the first set of wheels and tripped all over them. You and Nolen did amazing."

The wheels. They came before the ladder. Herja bit back a sigh as she finished her food. She hadn't gotten past the first task.

Wickham frowned and slid half of his sandwich to her.

She hesitated but took it. She was still starving!

"We could have done better," Nolen grumbled, looking unsettled.

"You did the best in the class," Wickham said, surprised. "Why do you think you should have done better?"

"I didn't say we should have—I said we could have," Nolen said.

Herja rolled her eyes. "That's the same thing. You're just trying to distract us now."

Nolen let out an aggravated sigh. "Our link only broke when I thought about how high I was—I let my fear of heights get the best of me. If I hadn't, the beam wouldn't have been a problem."

Herja lowered the half-sandwich Wickham had given her. "You're afraid of heights?"

Even as she blurted it out, she winced. That wasn't the sort of question you asked someone! He already said he was, she didn't have to double-down on it! However, Nolen didn't seem to be upset by her question.

"I am. I hate being off the ground, even so much as climbing a tree. The idea of being on a cliff for our afternoon class..." He shuddered. "The slope in that plank made it even."

"I didn't see it was sloped," Kaia said. "Not until after. If I had—"

Nolen closed his hand over hers, and an irrational jolt of jealousy went through her.

Penelope cleared her throat. "I'm pretty sure they put that slope there on purpose. So that it was something for the dragons to communicate with the witches. They're really pushing us, after all."

"I wish they hadn't," Nolen said, then shrugged. "But I guess that's part of the point, right? Pushing us to face our fears."

Herja looked up to the black clouds above the towering rock faces. Today the thunder hadn't been so bad so far, and she hadn't had to put on her earmuffs. It meant she didn't even have that as an excuse for failing the course so badly.

"I'm afraid of thunder," she said. Maybe admitting her own weakness would make up from her gaff earlier. "When I was younger, I'd hide underneath my bed with my hands over my ears every time it started to thunder and lightning."

"I didn't know that," Wickham said. His eyes were wide.

Herja wished he would take her hand like Nolen took Kaia's. But he kept his hands firmly on his half of the sandwich.

"Why did you think I wanted you to charm those earmuffs?" Herja asked, then cleared her throat. "Sorry, I didn't mean to sound so sulky."

"You didn't sound sulky," Wickham reassured her.

Herja wasn't sure she believed him, but she appreciated the effort, anyway. "When Mr. Bryce realized I was hiding every time it thundered, he put together a room in the basement where it was quieter and let me stay there whenever I wanted. He'd sing me songs like 'Five Little Frogs' and 'Mary Had a Little Lamb' until the storm passed.

Nolen smiled at her. "It sounds like he really cared about you."

"I..." Herja didn't know what to say about that, so she shoved the rest of her sandwich into her mouth.

Luckily, she didn't have to think of a way to respond. The bell rang, telling the students to reconvene. She quickly brushed the crumbs off herself and jumped to her feet.

"Thanks for the sandwich," she told Wickham.

The students gathered, and when everyone was back, Professor Gable took the witch students down the valley while Professor Delphine led the dragon students up the mountain. The day was hot and clear, and Herja was sweating before long.

It wasn't until they had already reached the cliff side and a distant rumble hit her ears that she had forgotten her earmuffs at camp. Her heart rate spiked, but she breathed deeply. No, she was going to get through this. The thunder wasn't loud and besides that; she had to overcome her fear.

She held her arms stiffly at her sides as Professor Delphine stepped to the edge of the cliff, standing before them. She would not let herself get overwrought just because there was a clap of thunder. Nolen was fine, and he was afraid of heights!

"Our dragons forms are a key part of our identity," Professor Delphine said. "When the sun created the first dragons, it was their duty to guard against the dangers of the world. This is still our mission, to defend those who cannot defend themselves."

Herja glanced upward again. Should she ask if she could run back to camp and get her earmuffs?

"You all know what dragons are capable of by this time. The key to the shift is learning how to be comfortable with a loss of control. Once you have that..." Professor Delphine grinned as she stepped backward...

... off the cliff.

The students all let out cries. Nolen darted forward as though he was going to catch her. He stumbled and Penelope leapt forward, grabbing the back of his shirt. She steadied him as a heavy beating sound filled the air.

Professor Delphine shot into the sky in her dragon form. She was a magnificent red-orange color, scales glittering like sparks in the sunlight. Her wings stretched out as she glided in a circle and came to land on the edge of the cliff, perching on her hind feet.

Her form seemed to ripple, like the reflection of a mirage, then she had returned to her human form.

The students all clapped. Herja followed suit, marveling. The professor had been so graceful! She flew through the air like she was dancing.

"Wings are the easiest thing a dragon can produce when shifting. Try not to focus too hard, think instead of flying and what that means to you," Professor Delphine said.

She moved through the students and spread them out so they each had space. Nolen, Herja saw, was placed near the back, away from the edge of the cliff. Odele, on the other hand, willingly moved to the edge.

Herja closed her eyes and tried to imagine herself flying, the way Professor Delphine had said. Her mind remained blank. How did people close their eyes and see images in her mind? Even her dreams seemed to be more something that she described to herself than 'saw' in the way it seemed like others did.

*What does flying mean to me? It means wind in my hair and on my face.*

A tingling formed between her shoulder blades. Herja's heart thudded, and she focused on that feeling, certain it was her wings—but the more she tried to concentrate, the harder that feeling became to find.

*Don't think too much,* she told herself.

But how did you stop thinking? Did you hum in your brain? How was that supposed to help with anything?

A gasp distracted her. Herja's head snapped up, and she gasped as well. Standing only a few feet from her was a dragon. Scales of turquoise-blue glittered, while a wingspan larger than that of any dragon relative to their size stretched out on either side of the dragon. A row of spikes ran down their neck, ending just before the wings, and picking up again near their hips to the tip of their tail.

"Well done, Penelope," Professor Delphine cried, clapping.

Herja clapped as well. Penelope held her dragon form for another few seconds before 'rippling' back to human form. Her red hair cascaded around her as she sat on the ground, panting.

"You did great!" Herja rushed to her friend and dropped to her knees to hug her tightly. "You're majestic. The prettiest dragon I've ever seen!"

Penelope hugged her back, beaming. "It's amazing. I can't describe what it feels like. But it's certainly taken a lot out of me."

Professor Delphine crouched near them and handed Penelope a waterskin. "Make sure you stay hydrated."

Herja hugged her friend again before she moved back to her spot. Seeing Penelope's dragon form only made her want to have that all the more. She closed her eyes. She could figure this out! She could learn how to be okay with a loss of control.

Somehow.

<hr />

WICKHAM HELD his hands over a small sage bush he'd found on the slope of the rocky valley. Around him, the other witches were holding rocks and twigs in their hands. They were all frowning and concentrating while the little bush he worked with danced merrily beneath his hands.

Wordless magic, as it turned out, was far easier to pick up than worded magic. At least, it was for him. His plant twined itself into a bundle, the easier to pick and dry. He grinned to himself. After having so much trouble last year with trying to use word-spells, he had worried about this year.

"Feel the energy within you and your target," Professor Gable instructed as he strode between the students. He paused near Kaia, who had thrown her rock to the ground in frustration. "If you're having a difficult time sensing anything, find a new way to come at the problem."

Kaia grunted and picked up a twig, glaring at it.

Professor Gable headed over to Wickham. "I see you've found something that works for you."

"Yes, sir," Wickham replied as he gingerly picked the sage twigs. "And sage is more than just a seasoning, there's any number of potions I can use it in."

"I see." Professor Gable picked up a small stone and pressed it into Wickham's hand. "Levitate this for me."

Wickham rolled the stone in his fingers, becoming used to the feeling of it in his palm. He held his hand out flat and imagined the stone rising a few inches. It twitched and rolled, seeming reluctant, but shakily rose a centimeter. He pictured it rising higher, and it did so, still slowly.

"Well done," Professor Gable said, sounding impressed.

Wickham allowed the stone to drop again. He grinned at the professor.

"Have you been taught how to use wordless magic when you worked in the hospital wing?" Professor Gable asked.

"Not exactly. I haven't been allowed to do more than prepare positions and tend to basic, minor injuries. But back home I helped the herbalist with a lot more. The village doesn't have a doctor, so it was just her and me," he explained. "And I guess I picked up on it by myself. I hope that will not cause any trouble."

Professor Gable shook his head. "Not trouble. I just need to know if I'm going to have to unteach you bad habits."

He gave Wickham a very pointed look which made Wickham wince. He hadn't picked up any bad habits, had he?

"I have had no formal work with wordless magic," Wickham hesitated, then sighed. "The first I can think of using it was in the Silent Marshes, when I was trying to keep Professor Lee alive after his head injury."

"I see. It seems you have already tapped into that part of you because of your challenges. With that in mind, I think we can move you to more advanced wordless magic," Professor Gable said.

Wickham swallowed hard. "But I did poorly last year."

"That was last year. I don't want to see you cannot reach your potential in this. Which means, for our classwork you will not work with grown plants."

Wickham's jaw dropped. That wasn't fair!

Professor Gable looked up at the other students. "Alright, that's enough for today. Take some time to rest in the shade and then head back to camp."

Wickham's hands tightened into fists. He wasn't angry so much as frustrated and confused. Why shouldn't he work with plants?

Professor Gable gestured for Wickham to come with him, then led him to another shady spot across the valley floor. It was well within sight of the others, but they wouldn't be able to hear the conversation.

"You are exceptionally talented in medicines and plant work, Wickham," the professor said, gazing up at the blue sky. "But you can't put all your self-esteem into one area like this. You're sabotaging yourself by focusing only on one aspect of your magic."

Wickham resisted the urge to roll his eyes. Why did all the adults think he didn't know himself? He had already decided on his future path, all he needed to know was healing magic and its offshoots.

Professor Gable peered at him shrewdly, like he was reading Wickham's mind, then hummed. "It's like this, Wickham. Think about your physical body. What's something in the morning workouts that you find easy?"

Wickham considered, then said, "Jumping jacks."

"There. So if you only ever did jumping jacks, would your muscles grow and develop?"

Wickham slowly shook his head.

"Now, what's your favorite book?" Professor Gable asked.

Wickham answered.

"Would you want to read nothing but that one book for the rest of your life?" Professor Gable gave him a stern look. "Or do you want to read more, to find other books that you enjoy, too?"

"I... don't understand how this has to do with my magic."

Professor Gable smiled at him. "You're limiting yourself. You aren't allowing your magic to fully grow. You're not letting yourself see if there are other uses for your magic that are enjoyable and fulfilling. Think about it. Just because you want to be a doctor doesn't mean you should ignore anything that isn't to do with medicine. We all need hobbies."

Wickham nodded slowly. He wasn't sure if he really understood or agreed with what the professor was saying, but it was something to think about, at least.

"Go on back to the others," Professor Gable said as he got to his feet. "Make sure you eat."

"Yes, Professor," Wickham replied, then jogged over to join the other witches.

So he wasn't allowed to work with plants during class. It was annoying, but he'd be fine. And he'd convince Professor Gable that he didn't need to have hobbies—herbalism was his hobby. What more did he need?

# CHAPTER

# SEVEN

THAT NIGHT AFTER CLASSES, Herja went to Professor Delphine's tent and asked to speak with her. The two sat outside at the small desk-and-table that was magically protected from the elements.

"The problem with these lessons are I don't understand what you're talking about," Herja started with no preliminary small talk. "For instance, earlier today you were telling us to think about what flying meant to us but at the same time, we're not supposed to think too much about it. So which is it?"

Professor Delphine crossed her ankles and folded her hands in her lap. "These instructions aren't meant to be taken literally, Herja. They're meant to guide you into a mindfulness of your body and the connection you have with your dragon form."

"Then why didn't you just tell us that?" Herja complained.

"I did. But you were too busy looking up at the mountain to hear." Professor Delphine gave her a small smile as Herja blushed. "Is there something you'd like to share? Some way I can help you, perhaps."

Herja mulled over the question. "I'm not sure. All I know is that this isn't working at all. I need something different."

"Different how?"

"I don't know."

Professor Delphine brushed her hair behind her ear. "Then exactly how am I meant to help, Herja? I'm not a mind reader."

Herja rubbed the back of her neck, thinking. Her lessons with Row had gone nowhere, either. They hadn't been able to teach her how to connect with her dragon. On the other hand, when they talked about connecting to her dragon, it made sense.

"Professor Farrow explains things to me," she said. "I need to understand the why in order to learn the how. They told me it's like holding your breath. It happens automatically and yet you control it, too."

"Professor Farrow is too indulgent with you."

Herja bristled at the implied insult in Professor Delphine's words. "They are not! They just want me to succeed and took the time to understand how to do that. Maybe if you took some time to figure out how to help me, you wouldn't be asking me to do your job—oh. No, I didn't mean that!"

She hid her face, her shoulders slumping forward. As upset as she was, there was no reason for her to lash out like this! Maybe it was because she was just extra tired and frustrated from failing to bring forward her dragon?

*Or maybe because I don't have control over my mouth and I'm always putting my foot in it.*

Herja peeked through her fingers. "I'm sorry. I didn't mean that. I'll take on extra camp duties in punishment. Do you think two or three days will be better?"

Hopefully two. She didn't want to have to do it three days in a row —but she would.

Professor Delphine, however, shook her head. She looked upset but not angry. "That will not be necessary. I spoke out of turn first and I can't expect a teenager to have better control of her emotions. I'm sorry. I shouldn't have said anything about Professor Farrow. I suppose as an orphan themself, they understand where you're coming from better."

"Row is an orphan?" Herja blurted. "Why didn't they tell me?"

Professor Delphine looked a little startled. "They didn't?"

"No, they didn't." Herja folded her arms, frowning. Why not?

"I'm sure they have their reasons."

Maybe they didn't want Herja to have unreasonable expectations about them? Herja swallowed hard. Over the past three years, she had gotten quite attached to her first-year professor. Maybe they wanted to make sure she understood there were boundaries in place, that they were only her teacher.

And maybe that was for the best, since Herja knew Row wasn't going to adopt her. If they were, they would have brought it up already, right?

"Farrow is quite private in their personal life," Professor Delphine said.

Herja shook her head. "Never mind. It isn't important."

"Hmm."

"The important thing here is that I have to understand why something works the way it does before I can start learning how to do it," Herja said, ignoring the shrewd look on her professor's face. "I've been that way all my life, so maybe I just have to learn this differently, too."

"Let's go to the well and draw some water," Professor Delphine said.

Why? Herja bit back the question as she followed the professor to the well.

"Your problem here is that you assume that this is something you have to learn how to do," Professor Delphine said as they drew water. "It doesn't work like that."

"It does for me."

"No. Not anymore than how you learned how to breathe in the first moments of life," Professor Delphine replied. "It's an instinct. Tap into it."

"But we have to learn *how* to do that," Herja argued.

"Perhaps," the professor said, inclining her head slightly.

Herja thought the response was cryptic. The professor asked her how she could help and now was ignoring her when she was trying to explain how she learned. Why was that?

"I'll give some more thought to our talk and see if I can figure out another way to approach it," Professor Delphine said as she dumped a bucket of water into their reserves. "Mostly though, dragons shift when they shift. There's no way to speed up the maturing process."

Herja nodded. Row told her that, too, and besides she didn't want to push her luck anymore.

"You should go get yourself some food now," the professor suggested. "It's been a long day."

"Thank you," Herja said automatically.

She headed toward the supply tent. They had only been given enough food to last them all to the end of the semester, which meant they had to stick to the rationing schedule strictly.

Maybe tomorrow she could convince Wickham and Nolen to go out into the forest with her to set some traps, so they could bulk up their supplies a bit... better to use what they could find and save these supplies in case of emergencies, right?

Kaia approached while she was fixing her food. "We're all heading down to the pond to swim a bit. Want to come?"

"No, thanks," Herja said. The sky was darkening with nighttime, not storm clouds, but she still didn't want to be anywhere near bodies of water. "I'm going to eat and get an early night."

"Alright. Hope you sleep well." Kaia hugged her. "Love ya."

"Love you, too," Herja said, a little awkwardly.

It was still strange to say it, though it was true. She did love her friends. Saying it out loud was weird, though.

After eating her supper rations, she cleaned up after herself and went to her tent. There, she found a letter on her pillow. Herja frowned as she picked it up. It was blank on both sides, so not something that had been delivered by the courier while they were at class today.

She hung her light stone lantern and opened the letter. The writing was smudged and hardly legible... but she could still read it.

And what she read made her heart nearly stop.

⁂

"WICKHAM!"

Wickham jerked upright, gasping. Where was he? Everything was dark. He'd been reading, hadn't he? When did it get so dark?

"Wick," the voice said again.

A glow spilled across his blankets as the tent flap was thrown back. The light stabbed violently into his eyes and Wickham threw an arm over his face, groaning. He recognized the voice now.

"Herja, you're not allowed here," he complained. "Our tents are only for one person, remember?"

"I need your help."

Wickham dropped his arm at once, his eyes widening. Herja, admitting that she needed help? He straightened and stared at her in concern and surprise. Had someone gotten hurt? Was someone dying? Were they being attacked?

Herja held a piece of paper up, then yanked it back when he reached for it.

"I got a letter from Raven."

"Raven?" Wickham repeated.

Herja let out a huff. "You know Raven."

Wickham scrubbed his hands over his face, trying to wake himself up. Herja talked so little of the orphanage that he was certain he'd remember a Raven, but he was drawing a blank.

"Who is she?"

"They," Herja corrected. "They're non-binary. They were a year older than me and came to the orphanage the same time I did. They were my friend until they got adopted. Remember?"

"Maybe, a little." Wickham finally got the sleep from his system and he crawled from his tent. Jerking his chin, he led Herja back to the sitting area, where they wouldn't get into trouble for being. "You said you wished they were part of the Silver Springs when we were first making the climb."

Herja nodded. "This is from them. They're here, somewhere on Thunder Ridge. The rumors about that new magical spring? It's true. They say that they found it and drank from it, but something terrible has happened. We need to go get them."

She turned, as though she was going to go gather her supplies right away. Wickham grabbed her wrist before she could get too far. "Wait! If someone is lost in the mountains, then we have to tell the professors."

Herja pulled herself free and shook her head. "No. They're not lost, Wick. They left the letter on my pillow, which means they've been around long enough to know which tent is mine. If they wanted the adults involved, they would have revealed themselves before now."

"But we can't go out by ourselves."

"Why not? Raven told me where to meet them. Once I find out what's going on and what this terrible thing they talked about is, then we can figure out if we can bring them back or not."

Wickham had never seen Herja so... well, *desperate*. She held herself so still, like she was trying to prevent herself from flying every which way all at once. Her tone was pleading and demanding both.

"What about rocs?" he tried. His gut clenched; what were the chances that Herja's one friend before coming to the Institute would be here, in the Storm Mountains? And then to say that these magical spring rumors were true?

It didn't seem real. But who would possibly want to trick her?

*It could be Odentia, wanting to kidnap her.*

"They only come out with the worst storms and we've got stars. Look! There won't be a major storm tonight." Herja's expression was not as confident as her words as she looked above them.

Wickham seized on this chance. "But there might be a storm. Since Raven has been here for so long, it means they know how to get here and where to take shelter, right? So if there is a storm, they'll be able to retreat to safety. We don't know these mountains."

Herja's gaze dropped back to him. "Why are you being so stubborn? I came to you to ask for help, not to be chastised! Raven asked me for my help. I can't let them down."

"I'm not trying to be stubborn."

"Good! Then get some supplies and we'll head out. Raven must be starving."

Wickham groaned. That's not what he meant at all! How was he going to get through to her? "You don't even know it's from Raven. It could be someone from Odentia—"

"Odentia and Eldavon are working peacefully together, they have no reason to attack and even if they did, no reason to come after me personally," Herja snapped.

"Maybe it's another thing like last year with the Chameleon Sprites—"

"It's not. Row would have told me."

Wickham combed his fingers through his long hair. "Herja... I'm not saying you absolutely shouldn't go. But you shouldn't tonight. Please. Sleep on it and let's revisit tomorrow morning?"

Herja dropped back a step. Her expression closed off, but her shoulders slumped. "Tomorrow."

"Just until morning," Wickham pleaded.

Her hands clenched and released. "Fine," she snapped, then turned on her heel.

"Herja," he called after her, but she didn't turn back around. His stomach still tied into knots as she returned to her side of the tents. She was going to listen to him, right?

She wouldn't head up the mountain by herself at night...

Right?

# CHAPTER
# EIGHT

PENELOPE TOWELED OFF HER HAIR, feeling more relaxed than she had in quite a while. Swimming was always good for her muscles and emotions. She'd have to remember that in the future.

She grinned to herself as she wrapped the towel up around her head and pulled her nightclothes out of her bag, careful not to drip too much on them. Her dragon was beautiful. Everyone said so. And she was the first in the year to fully shift. Maybe when Julie said she'd find her mate eventually, she was right. Maybe there wasn't anything wrong with her after all.

"Penelope," Wickham's voice came from outside the tent. "I need to talk to you!"

Penelope frowned. She was still in her swimming suit, so she slithered out of the tent and faced Wickham. He carried a light stone lantern, his eyes wide.

"What's wrong?" Penelope whispered, trying not to disturb the others. Wickham wouldn't have come over to the girls' side of the camp without reason.

"Herja's gone."

Penelope's gut clenched. *"What?"*

Wickham hurriedly explained about Raven's letter and his argument with Herja. The guilt and regret were clear on his face.

"Get Kaia and Nolen, get them to meet us at the supply tent," Penelope said, her mind zeroing in on the problem.

Clearly, Herja had gone off by herself to meet Raven. Which meant they had to find her and bring her back, before she got into more trouble. It was clear as day Herja chaffed under Professor Delphine's instructions, the last thing Penelope wanted was to make it worse.

So, they'd have to go get her back.

Wickham nodded and hurried off. Penelope dove back into her tent and changed into dry clothes that would keep her warm in the mountains, then rolled up her bedroll and put it into her pack.

With any luck, they wouldn't need it. But just in case, she'd bring it.

Soon, she and the others were at the supply tent. Kaia looked worried as Penelope and Wickham explained the situation. When they were done, she glanced at the professors' tents.

"Shouldn't we tell them?" she asked anxiously.

Penelope shook her head. "Herja shuts down too easily. Especially with what happened last year, I don't want to break her trust unless it's absolutely necessary. We'll probably catch up with her soon enough, anyway."

Nolen nodded his agreement. "Kaia, you've gotten good at parsing out tracks when we were in the Silent Marshes over the summer. You can show us where she went and when we catch up, we can get a better picture of them."

"Exactly," Penelope said. "Wickham, when was your talk with Herja?"

"About half an hour, I think."

Penelope pulled her pack off and started selecting some of the prepped meal kits, the sort that you only had to add water to.

"If Raven has been hiding out here for a while, they're going to be hungry. So let's all make sure our water skins are full and I'll bring a couple of these so they can have some food. I also want us to have our knives on us."

She grabbed a few bags of nuts for the team to snack on. They group hurried to the pumping station and filled their water skins, and soon were heading out. Penelope listened to the familiar sounds of the forest.

Unlike the swampy green jungle of the Silent Marshes and the magnificent oaks and birches of the Golde Forest, here on Thunder Ridge most trees were the sort that survived in temperate regions. Pines, spruces, the occasional fir. It was the type of forest she was used to.

"If the professors find out we've snuck away, we're going to be in big trouble," Kaia murmured as they headed toward the path.

"I'll think of something," Penelope said. "Kaia, you're up."

Kaia took her wand out and pointed it at the ground. She turned it over in her hand for a moment before she chanted, "Mary had a little lamb but Herja is our friend. Show us where her footprints start and lead us to where they end."

Thunder growled overhead, making them all flinch and look up. Penelope searched the darkness overhead. There was hardly a star in the sky anymore. Was it because of storm clouds or normal cloud cover?

When she looked back down, a single set of footprints glowed in a faint orange light on the ground, leading up the side of the mountain.

"Stay together. Wickham, you lead the way," Penelope said. Wick had the least endurance in their group when it came to inclined trails. She took up the back as the thunder grew even louder.

Herja was going to be terrified of this. Would she be afraid enough to turn around and head back to camp? Hopefully...

But Penelope didn't think so. If anything was going to make Herja face her fear or thunderstorms, it was her sheer stubbornness.

They had to find her before it started to rain. Otherwise, they'd lose her tracks.

*Don't think about it. We'll find her. We have to.*

KAIA'S SPELL unfortunately only lasted about forty-five minutes before it failed. She groaned as the orange illumination disappeared yet again. This was the fourth time she had cast the spell. Or was it the fifth? She'd completely lost track.

She pointed her wand at the ground. "Herja is lost. Track her."

No point in using the fancier rhymes this time. They hadn't exactly helped make it last longer before. The prints flared to a ghostly green.

"What does that mean?" Nolen demanded, worried.

"It means it's the dead of night and I'm not sure how much longer I can keep going," Kaia replied exhaustedly. "Wick, when these die I'm going to need you to try again."

Wickham glanced back. In the light of the lantern Penelope carried, Kaia could see the frustration in his eyes. He had tried before, to no avail. He could usually muddle through word-based magics, but this apparently was too much for him.

They were all exhausted, too. After how many hours walking through the forest, Kaia fluctuated between anger at Herja for leaving, anger at Penelope for not letting them tell the professors, anger at herself for not ignoring Penelope, and a deep fear that paralyzed her lungs.

"We should have found her by now," Nolen grumbled as they continued on. "She's not this fast, is she? Especially in the dark."

"Herja is the fastest out of all of us, except Pen," Wickham replied. Despite the tiredness in his voice, the fear was still clear. "But only over short distances. Even Pen doesn't have Herja's endurance."

Kaia stumbled forward. The tip of her wand lit the way, but either the light was dimming or her eyes were growing moss. She stifled a yawn as she reached for her waterskin. Maybe if she just got a little hydration—

The light from her wand landed on an enormous creature in the path ahead and she dropped it, screaming.

Nolen grabbed her protectively and put her behind him. Penelope rumbled, the sound like a dragon as she leapt forward, brandishing the lantern in one hand and her knife in the other. She stopped though as the creature remained still. Like a statue.

Kaia picked up her wand again and added its light to the lantern. She gasped. It was a white-tailed deer, a stag with four points on each antler.

It was stone.

Every strand of fur stood in perfect order, its eyes huge. It was as though someone had taken a living creature and turned it into rock.

A chill stole down Kaia's spine. That was exactly what happened.

"This is magic," Wickham breathed. He drew closer to the others. "Someone did this."

"You mean a *person*?" Nolen demanded.

Wickham nodded. "I can't tell you how, but the energy is..."

"Off," Kaia finished for him. "It's not like anything I've sensed before. This was a living thing. Maybe it even still is. I don't know. It's just... wrong."

Penelope cleared her throat and stepped around the stag. "Let's keep going."

Kaia wanted nothing more than to just turn around and go back to the camp. It was bad enough trying to make their way through the darkness like this, but now that they ran into this? The hairs on her arms and neck stood on end and she couldn't stop shivering, even when Nolen put an arm around her.

"We can go back," he said.

Another crack of thunder peeled overhead. Kaia flinched and pressed herself tighter into Nolen's side. The steps where Herja had walked glowed a little brighter. It occurred to Kaia that Herja would have seen this as well. She would flinch even more with each burst of thunder.

"No. Herja's out there and she needs us. We're her friends, we can't let her down," Kaia said. She pulled away from her perfect match and gave him a wobbly sort of smile. "We have to keep going."

A few meters further along the path was a doe. Her legs were bent as though she was getting ready to bolt when she had been turned into stone. It made Kaia's heart ache to see it.

What if the same thing happened to Herja? What if they came across her as a statue?

Kaia couldn't bear to think about it and pushed herself to walk faster.

After half an hour, the path died.

"Wick?" Kaia asked warily.

He knelt in the lantern's light and pressed his fingers into the ground, "Show us the tracks."

At first there was nothing. Then a bluish light glowed from the ground, showing Herja's tracks once more. Only they weren't alone. Another set coincided with Herja's. These were larger by at least two inches. An adult?

Kaia's mind flashed to Finnegan. He had escaped from prison—but surely, he couldn't be here!

Maybe Raven just had big feet.

But Wick was worried the letter was fake.

Kaia clenched her jaw to keep her fears to herself. All that mattered right now was they find Herja. As to who was following and turning these creatures into stone? They'd deal with that once they knew Herja was safe. And if it was Finnegan... she wasn't a scared little girl anymore.

She was growing into her magic, and she had her mate. Finnegan would learn it was unwise to mess with them again.

# CHAPTER
# NINE

WICKHAM'S HEAD JERKED UP, making his neck kink. He groaned as he rubbed his sore muscles. He was so tired! He was practically falling asleep as they walked. His legs were on fire, his feet so long past pain they were numb. The waterskin strap had worn the skin raw where it rubbed on his neck.

"We'll take a five-minute break," Penelope called. Even though she had been doing her best to keep them animated, Wickham could hear the exhaustion in her voice as well.

The night was so deep and black that the light stone lantern barely illuminated the surrounding space. Kaia had had to extinguish her wand long ago so she could use the walking stick Nolen had found for her.

Wickham didn't want to stop to rest, but seeing his friends in their current state forced him to keep that to himself.

"I should have gone to the professors," he moaned as he sank to the ground. It was damp and cold, but he didn't care. He rested his head on his arm.

A fat drop of water hit his forehead. Then another.

He turned over, trying to ignore it. It must just be a heavy mist—

Lightening lit up the area, illuminating everything in perfect clarity. Half a second later, thunder boomed so loudly it seemed to shake the ground. In the next second, a torrential downpour had blinded him. He shouted but the noise of the rain was so loud he couldn't hear if anyone answered.

Another flash of lightening and he lunged for the streak of red hair in the rain. He grabbed Penelope's arm as the thunder deafened him. Clasping her hand in his, he lifted his other one and felt out a spell, searching for Kaia and Nolen. He led Penelope to them, and the four joined hands, forming a chain.

After that, Wickham wasn't sure who was leading them, only that someone was.

The rain cut out abruptly, though the noise was still deafening. The lantern emerged through the rain behind him. They were in a cave that appeared to go deep enough to escape from the wind. The four students hurried into the back when suddenly Nolen stopped them.

"Who's there?" he yelled.

Penelope lifted the lantern higher. The light fell on a shivering form at the back of the cave. It was inky black and when another peel of thunder deafened them; it curled into a tighter ball.

Herja!

"Kaia, can you muffle the entrance?" Wickham asked as he pushed past Nolen. He threw himself down next to Herja and wrapped his arms around her. "Herja! Herja, it's us. Wick, Pen, Kaia and Nolen. You're okay."

Herja's arms wrapped around him. She buried her face into his chest and clung to him so tightly it hurt his ribs. Another peel of thunder, this one not so deafening.

Mr. Bryce would sing to her. Singing! He could do that.

What were some of Herja's favorite songs? Oh! He knew.

*"Are you going to Scarborough fair?"* he sang. *"Parsley, sage, rosemary and thyme?"*

Kaia knelt beside them and put her hand on Herja's back, rubbing gently as she joined in. *"Remember me to one who lives there."*

*"She once was a true love of mine,"* they sang together.

Penelope and Nolen both started to 'set camp'. They strung a blanket from one side of the cave to the other, blocking out the wind and rain. Nolen crept over and crouched next to the group, a waterskin in his hands.

*"Tell her to make me a cambric shirt. Parsley, sage, rosemary and thyme..."*

Penelope shook out another blanket and draped it over Wickham's shoulders. The warmth immediately seeped through his wet clothes. Penelope then gave another one to Kaia and Nolen and put a third over Herja before she dug into the pack again.

By the time they reached the end of the song, Penelope was trying to make a fire. Nolen tucked the blanket around Kaia and went to help her.

Wickham started the song over. Herja was slowly relaxing. She no longer shook so constantly, but her grip on him hadn't loosened. He stroked her wet hair while Kaia continued to rub her back soothingly.

Eventually, Herja lifted her face. Her eyes were red and puffy as she looked up into Wickham's eyes.

His heart seized to see her look so vulnerable. His arms tightened around her.

"You came looking for me?" Her voice was hoarse.

"Of course," Wickham said.

Penelope made a disgruntled noise as she and Nolen finally got the fire going. "We thought you had been kidnapped."

Wickham glared at Penelope.

"What?" Pen glared right back. "We were all thinking it! We thought someone had attacked you or kidnapped you. What were you thinking, taking off like that in the middle of the night?"

Nolen laughed—actually laughed! Wickham's jaw tightened until the other boy talked.

"I think it's for the same reason we all took off in the middle of the night, Penelope," he said with a wry shake of his head. "Because when a friend is in trouble... we dragons don't stop to think about all the complications. We just want to find our friend and make it better."

Herja adjusted her position, so she was sitting on her own, though she kept her cheek pressed into Wickham's chest. "We're friends?"

"Yes."

"But we don't tell each other secrets," Herja said with a frown.

Nolen shrugged. "So we're not close friends. You don't have to have all or nothing, friendship is a spectrum."

Herja smiled, then buried her face into Wickham's chest again as the thunder grew louder.

"Let's try to get some food heated," Penelope said as she dug into her pack again. "And then we could all use some sleep."

***

PENELOPE FOUGHT the yawn that threatened to crack her jaw as she brought the pan of water back in from filling it up in the rain. It had only taken five minutes. The blanket she had put up to block out the wind was soaked through, dripping into the cave now, but the back of the cave where the fire was remained dry.

Nolen had built a small space for the pan and Penelope wiped the bottom off before putting it on. She was grateful for Nolen's help. Wick, Herja, and Kaia were amazing troopers, but they didn't know forest living like she did. It was nice that this time it wasn't all on her shoulders.

"We should try to dry out our clothes," Nolen said, frowning around at the cave. "Maybe we can make a clothesline across here in front of the fire. Wickham and I could dry our shirts out first and then switch it out. Or we could all just forget about modesty for the sake of survival. I'm comfortable with just our underclothes but..."

He shrugged.

Penelope smirked at him. "In the Fire Watch, we don't think too much about various shades of nudity, either. Kind of hard to be embarrassed when it's simple prudence."

"But they're not from the Watches like us."

"I can hear you." Herja pulled away from Wickham and groped behind her. "I brought blankets and clothes, too. I ensured I had a waterproof bag so they should still be dry. So if we can't all have dry clothes, we at least can wrap up in blankets. I'm not saying there's anything wrong with unclothed bodies," she added as she dug into her pack. "But it's wiser to be covered up to stay warm."

Herja had brought two sets of clothing. One for her, and one for Raven. Penelope, Kaia, and Nolen were all too big for her clothes, so Herja changed into one dry set and Wickham wore the other. Penelope took one of the dry blankets to a corner and took off her soaking over-clothes, then used the blanket to cover herself up like a toga.

Herja, seeming much better now, helped to string up their clothes-line and hang the clothes while Kaia watched over the food.

By the time they were done with the clothes, the water was boiling and the food was ready.

"I tell you, food never tastes better than when we're in a situation like this," Penelope said as she dug into her bowl

"I know," Kaia sighed. "I love food but boy oh boy! Something about being exhausted really brings out the appetite."

She laid her head on Nolen's shoulder. Both of them wore their blankets like togas, too, and Kaia had an extra one wrapped around her so it looked like she was wearing an overdress.

Wickham and Herja were sitting together, too. One couple on one side of the fire, the other on the other. And Penelope was just far enough from both of them not to feel like she was part of the group.

She lowered her head and concentrated on her food. Eat, sleep, and figure out what happened next. No time to waste feeling sorry for herself.

⁂

AFTER ONLY A FEW bites of the food, Herja felt her eyes drooping. She felt weak and shivery, but the warmth of the food in her belly made her think maybe she could stay asleep if she actually fell asleep. Kaia's spell to keep the thunder at bay was working. It wasn't nearly as dangerous now.

Her head fell to Wickham's shoulder and her eyes drooped.

"Penelope?" Kaia said suddenly, jerking Herja back to the cave. Kaia's eyebrows pinched together, worry in her clear eyes. "Are you okay?"

Hera glanced at Penelope. Shock washed over her as Penelope wiped a tear from her eye. Was she really serious when she said she thought Herja had been kidnapped?

"It's fine," Penelope said. Her voice was thick.

"No, it's not." Herja straightened. "Is it my fault?"

Penelope gave her a startled look. She wiped her face again, then lowered her gaze to the fire. "No. It's not your fault. It's not anyone's fault."

"Are you crying because you were worried about me?" Herja pressed. "Did you get hurt? Did—"

"No! It's just that... well, look at us. One set of mates here, the other there," she gestured first to Herja and Wickham, then Kaia and Nolen. "And here I am, alone. I'm trying to accept it. I'm trying to keep positive and sometimes I even think maybe it's okay to be different like this. But it hurts. I want a mate!"

She wrapped her arms around herself, her lip trembling.

Herja clutched at her bowl, silent. She wanted to say something to make her feel better. But what could she say? The only thought that came to her was that the stars must have chosen it to be this way for a reason.

But the platitude felt empty. What reason could they have to put Penelope through this pain?

"I can't help but feel like maybe there's something wrong with me, that's why I wasn't given a mate. And when I see the connection between all of you... I'm jealous. I have to admit it. I just wish I knew why."

Why. It was what Herja wanted to know, too. Why things happened the way they did, why things worked like this or that.

Why she wasn't adopted.

Why her brain didn't seem to work like other people's.

Why she couldn't seem to make herself open up to her connection with Wickham. Why she could long to make him happy but be frozen in the not knowing what to do.

Maybe it was because she wasn't sure what she wanted with a relationship with him.

Maybe it was because something was wrong with her, too.

She inhaled deeply. "I thought there was a mistake. On the night of the celebration."

Penelope turned to her, her eyes still damp. "What?"

"When I saw you didn't have a mate. I thought something went wrong. And when I realized Wickham was mine... I thought I had somehow stolen your mate from you. Because you already had such a connection to him," Herja said, her voice shaking. She glanced at Wickham to find his expression stunned.

"You don't want me?" he asked.

Herja shook her head. "It's not that at all. You're my best friend. I just thought... I couldn't understand why Pen didn't have a mate." A thought occurred to her, and she breathed out a deep breath. "But I think, maybe I figured it out."

Penelope stared at her.

"You did already have a connection with Wick," Herja said slowly. "And you have a connection with Kaia. Every witch you're paired with, you are able to easily have some level of mind-to-mind communication. And just look at what happened when we went to the Silver Springs."

"What do you mean?" Penelope asked.

Herja smiled softly at her, pieces she didn't even know were there falling into place. "You automatically became our leader. There was no reason for us all to defer to you, and yet we did. Maybe you don't have a mate because your connections run deeper. You're able to connect to everyone on some level. Maybe that's why."

Penelope wiped her face. "It sounds nice, at least. Thank you."

Herja nodded at her. They resumed eating. But when Herja glanced at Wickham, she couldn't help but think he looked hurt. Had she pushed him further away in her attempts to comfort Penelope?

# CHAPTER
# TEN

KAIA SLEPT RESTLESSLY. The thunder kept going, and she had to restore her spell every hour until just after dawn. It was only then that she actually slept hard. Even though she considered herself something of a night owl, this was too much.

Nolen, of course, was the first one to wake up. He woke her up first. "The sun is out, we can figure out what to do next."

Her body still ached, but Kaia pulled herself to a sitting position. The kink in her neck was giving her a headache and she rubbed at it as she got her bearings. The cave was actually much shallower than she had thought the previous night, but the back here was dipped upward so that the puddles of water drained out of it.

Her clothes weren't fully dry, but by this time her blanket-toga was just as damp. She got dressed stiffly, hissing in pain as her muscles protested.

Once everyone was awake and things were packed up, the group moved to the mouth of the cave. Outside the day was hot and humid. Muggy.

"We should go back to camp," Kaia said, rubbing her neck again. "They'll know we're gone by now and after that storm, everyone will be worried. We're going to be in a lot of trouble."

"You can go back if you want." Herja said. "But Raven is still out there. I'm going to find them."

Kaia's shoulders slumped, which only pulled on her neck muscles more. She had suspected that Herja wouldn't be satisfied. Despite the dangers that they faced now, Herja wasn't the sort of person to ask for help.

"I don't think it's a good idea to separate. You saw the deer turn into stone?" Kaia asked.

Herja's steely eyes stared out at the dripping forest. "Those were just statues."

"No, it was magic. Someone turned them into stone. The more eyes we have, the better protected we'll be against attack," Kaia said. "And the professors are more experienced—"

Herja's head snapped around. She glared at Kaia. "I'm not leaving my friend out here alone. Like you said, the fewer people there are, the more likely we are to be attacked. Raven is alone. They need help."

Kaia turned to Nolen beseechingly. If anyone was going to back her up, it would be her mate, right?

"We'll have to see if we can even find the trail, still," Nolen said, striding out of the cave. His gaze was on the ground. "That storm will have washed most of it away, but if Kaia and Wickham can light up Raven's trail like they did for you, we'll be able to find them."

Kaia's heart crashed down.

Penelope and Herja both joined Nolen.

"Where was Raven supposed to meet you?" Penelope asked.

"Here, according to their note. When the storm started, I tried to go out and look for them but... I couldn't." Herja hung her head.

Kaia and Wickham glanced at each other. If they both refused to use their magic to track Raven, then the five of them would have no choice but to head back to camp. But would Herja forgive them for that? Or would she just head out with no idea of where to find Raven at all?

"Raven might have been injured in the storm," Nolen called over his shoulder. "I think I see something—a cloak, maybe?"

The three dragons headed down the steep, muddy mountainside.

"Maybe we'll find Raven soon," Wickham murmured. "Herja will not leave the mountain without them."

He went after the others, leaving Kaia to pick her way along behind them miserably. Of course she didn't want to leave someone out here potentially injured, but it just seemed far too unwise to figure this all out by themselves!

By the time Kaia caught up with them, the movement had worked out most kinks and pain in her muscles. The others had also found a blood-stained cloak.

"Look at this track," Nolen said, pointing to upturned dirt and broken scrub brush. "Someone fought here. After the storm stopped, it looks like. And we're not that far from the cave."

Kaia's skin prickled. Did that mean someone could have crept in on them while they were sleeping? Could they have been attacked? "Maybe it was a couple of animals?"

"No. Look, there are boot prints," Penelope pointed out, then bent. "And knives. There were at least two people here."

"One of them has to be Raven." Herja hurried forward and took the knives. She turned them over in her hand, then gave a stifled gasp.

Her gaze flickered up to Kaia, which only made the prickling of her skin worse. She took a deep breath. "They're Odentian blades, aren't they?"

"How can you tell?" Wickham asked.

"By the way Herja's looking at me," Kaia replied. She turned to the other witch, her face set. "Finnegan escaped from prison. He was obsessed with finding magic. I thought he'd have been caught by now. Or at the very least that he wouldn't be able to get here."

Nolen took her hand and squeezed. "There's no proof it's him."

"Doesn't matter," Kaia said, straightening her shoulders. She pulled her wand from the pouch at her waist and pointed it at the ground. "Show us where Raven went."

AN HOUR FOLLOWING Raven's trail and they came across more creatures turned into stone and another scuffle. Several dark stains in the earth looked like blood. Wickham watched Herja's face carefully. Though the grim determination in her eyes never faded, a hopelessness seemed to come over her.

"Someone was injured," Nolen said. He stared at one statue, another white-tailed deer. "Do you think Finnegan found the springs? He seems like the type that would abuse his powers and do this."

"We can't just assume it's Finnegan," Penelope said. "It could be someone more dangerous. Or it could be several people. We don't know, it's a mistake to pretend like we do."

Herja flinched at Penelope's words. Wickham reached for her hand, wanting to comfort her, but she pulled away and shied from him.

"Let's keep moving," she snapped, clearly unnerved. "Kaia?"

"Wait." Kaia was peering deeply into the eye of the stone deer.

"No, no waiting," Herja said, striding over to her. "We have to find Raven! Don't you understand? Finnegan could turn them into stone!"

Penelope made a strangling noise in her throat.

Wickham stepped for Herja, reaching for her again. "I'm sure Raven will be fine—"

"You don't know that!"

"Quit arguing," Kaia snapped. She touched her fingers to the forehead of the buck. "Everyone be quiet. They're still alive. I'm sure of it. I can feel the energy in them. Which means maybe I can save them."

Herja dug her fingers into her inky hair. "Kaia—"

"Which means—" Kaia continued.

Penelope finished. "If Raven was turned to stone, you will be able to save them, too."

"Exactly. We should try at least, right?" Kaia asked. She looked between Herja and Penelope. Nolen hovered behind her, looking anxious.

Wickham frowned. Something was off about this magic, though. They didn't know how Kaia's magic would interact with it. He reached out, trying to sense the lingering energies in the earth and around them.

Something tickled the back of his mind. As the pulses of energy reached the base of the first statue, it was as though his throat closed over. He gasped soundlessly, trying to get air.

"Restore—" Kaia began, her wand pointed at the buck.

Wickham threw himself forward on instinct. He tackled her around the waist, knocking her over. The two tumbled over the sharp, stony ground as Kaia cried out. She pushed him off as they came to a stop.

"What are you doing?"

"I'm sorry! But I just knew—it feels wrong. I touched it with magic, wordless magic, and I—" Wickham held up his hands, cutting himself off.

The tips of his fingers were grey stone. He gasped and Kaia clapped both hands to her mouth. The stony color slowly retreated to his pink tones. He flexed his fingers, feeling dizzy and lightheaded. He was just able to turn away to vomit into a bush, rather than all over Kaia. Once he was done, he collapsed onto the cool earth.

"What happened?" Penelope demanded.

"He was turning into stone. I think... I think that's what would have happened, if I tried to use my magic. I would have..." Kaia trailed off.

Hands grabbed hold of Wickham and turned him. He groaned, but when he saw it was Herja, he tried to bite down on his feelings of weakness. She helped him to a sitting position and gave him water, but didn't linger.

Instead, she returned to the statues and touched one of the doe's ears. "We're taking too long. We're too slow."

Penelope put a hand on Herja's shoulder. "We're going as fast as we can. We'll find Raven, Herja. I promise."

Herja's head bent but she nodded.

Wickham sipped the water he still had, his thoughts all awhirl. This was above their abilities. He couldn't keep going, and by the look on Kaia's face, she wouldn't be able to either. And yet he couldn't leave Herja out here by herself, either.

What was he going to do?

# CHAPTER
# ELEVEN

THERE WASN'T a trace of blue in the sky.

Penelope pushed her hair from her face. Despite the cloud cover, the day was hot and muggy, and there were mosquitoes aplenty out. None of Nolen's tricks to deter them worked... not that the bugs were Penelope's actual concerns here.

"The tracks go through here," Herja said.

She was a few meters ahead of them and often stopped just long enough for them to catch up with her before speeding on ahead again. Penelope had stopped trying to keep her with the group, even though she was certain Herja would be less impatient if she stayed with them.

Her black hair was spiked up all around her from the many times she ran her hand through it. Her silver eyes, normally calm, were wild with impatience and fear.

Herja disappeared through a group of wild roses, but Nolen rounded them and called out, "Come this way, it's easier." The tracks continued heading up the mountain.

Wickham and Kaia shared an exhausted sort of look.

"Let's keep moving," Penelope encouraged them under her breath. "The spell won't last much longer."

They nodded and hurried to join Nolen and Herja. Penelope

followed them, keeping an eye not only on the group but also on the surrounding forest. With whoever was turning creatures into stone out there, they couldn't be too careful.

In all honesty, continuing like this wasn't a wise decision. It would be far smarter to go back down the mountain, return to camp, and get help to keep going.

However, she knew there was no way Herja would accept that course of action. She'd already proven that, so the best next thing was to find Raven so they could all go down together.

When the magic dissolved off the footprints, she called for a rest.

Herja glared at her, but Penelope jerked her chin to Kaia and Wickham. The two witches had sunk to the ground and were currently mopping sweat off their faces and necks.

"We must be getting closer now," Herja thought. "If we hurry, we'll be able to catch them in no time."

Though Penelope knew she was trying to be encouraging, her words only caused their companions to look more agitated.

"Let us sit for five minutes before you try to push us on," Kaia complained.

"I'm not pushing," Herja protested.

Wickham shook his head. "You are pushing."

Penelope quickly cleared her throat loudly. "Herja, can we talk privately, please?"

"About what?"

"Something private," Penelope said cagily.

Herja's jaw clenched, but she nodded and followed Penelope aside. They kept close enough to see the others but far enough that their conversation wouldn't travel.

"I have a few things to say," Penelope said in a low voice. "First, Kaia and Wick aren't mad at you."

Herja's scowl grew deeper. "No? You really don't think so?"

"I know they aren't. They're scared, exhausted and trying to fight through it for your sake. What looks like anger is just them not having any energy to spare to mask." Penelope let that sink in for Herja, then continued. "That being said, we can't keep dragging them around this mountain."

"I'm not—"

Penelope lifted one hand. "Please?"

Herja huffed but nodded as she fell silent.

"We can't risk the group separating, not when we could each be in greater danger. The truth is, though, Raven is faster than we are. And we're getting slower every hour. We need to find out how fresh the tracks are. They could be from days ago," Penelope said, trying to keep her voice firm enough to convey the importance of her words while also soft enough to be sympathetic.

Herja drew a hand through her black hair.

"We've had storm clouds all day," Penelope continued. "We do not know when we'll get another storm. We're all in greater danger if we don't find Raven before the next wave. And I know you're fine taking on the risk yourself... but what about Wick and Kaia?"

Herja's response was to kick the ground. But she wasn't scowling anymore, which was a hopeful sign.

Penelope waited a moment, letting her words sink in before she sighed. "I know you don't want to wait. But at this point, I think we have to admit that we need help. Once at camp, Professor Delphine can fly back to this spot, and we'll have the entire year to help. Professor Gable's magic is far stronger than Kaia and Wickham's."

"So, what you're saying," Herja started, "is that if we have more help, we will have a better chance at finding Raven. That going back isn't giving up, but acknowledging that the situation is bigger than the five of us?"

"That's exactly what I'm saying," Penelope said, relieved.

"And by having more of us looking for Raven, there's less chance that they or we will be harmed."

Penelope nodded. "Professor Gable can put protective wards over us to prevent whoever's been attacking the deer from getting us, too."

Herja's chin dropped to her chest as she pinched her eyes shut. She looked like she might reconsider the situation, which Penelope counted as a good sign.

"I just don't like the idea of Raven out here," Herja finally whispered. "If I had to guess someone they would contact for help, I'd be the last person on the list. It's my fault we fell out of contact in the first place."

Penelope reached to hug her friend, fully expecting Herja would slip away.

To her surprise, Herja accepted the embrace and hugged her back tightly. "I just want my friend back, and I don't know what else I'm supposed to do."

"I know."

It was a terrible position to be in. Penelope tried to think about what she'd do if any of her friends were lost out here.

But she did know. She had been part of the Fire Watch long enough to know that having a one-person search party wasn't good enough when it came to someone being lost in the wilderness. If someone got lost, the entire camp mobilized to find them.

"We will get back to camp, and then we can get help to find Raven," Penelope said again, more firmly this time. "This is too big for us."

Wickham suddenly cried out.

Both Herja and Penelope whipped around. Wickham and Kaia were on their feet, with Nolen protectively standing before them.

Herja raced forward. Scales appeared over her arms and the back of her neck. They shimmered in the dim light as she planted herself next to Nolen.

Penelope was slower than the other two. She scanned the area behind them, ensuring nobody was coming at the group from behind. Her hands curled into fists as she checked for any sign of danger.

A small figure stumbled from the woods.

Their clothes were soaked, clinging to a thin frame. They wore a hood that hid their hair, and a ragged scarf covered their face like a funeral shroud. One hand held the scarf in place over their face, while the other clung to a stick they used to prop themself up.

The five students froze, staring at the newcomer.

Penelope stepped forward and stopped. Something was... wrong. She couldn't put her finger on it.

But something was wrong.

HERJA'S HANDS curled and uncurled at her sides as she narrowed her eyes, peering at the figure as they slumped to their knees. Part of her wanted to run forward and catch them, but another part held back.

They might be Raven...

Or they might be the person turning creatures into stone.

The figure lifted its shrouded face, and Herja fell back a step. Something felt off about the situation. It was like when you bit into a strawberry and couldn't quite tell if it had turned bad. You were caught in that half-second between spitting it out or chewing.

"Herja?" a thin voice said.

The tension broke. "Raven!"

She started forward, but Raven dropped their walking stick and held up their hand. "No, no, stay back. Don't come near me."

Herja ignored them until Wickham grabbed her arm.

"Raven, what's wrong?" Herja asked urgently. "We're here to help."

"Something terrible happened." Raven sounded like they were on the verge of tears.

Penelope stepped to one side, a frown on her face. "What is it? Are you being hunted?"

Raven's head turned toward Penelope. "I only contacted Herja so she could stop it from happening again."

"Are you being hunted?" Herja repeated.

Raven let out a huff. "Maybe. But that's not the important part right now. You've heard about the rumors, the second spring that grants magical powers?"

Herja nodded, then added, "Yes," in case Raven couldn't see her through that shroud.

"It's true," Raven said. They sank to their knees, shivering.

Kaia dug into the pack, pulled out a blanket, and started forward. Nolen stopped her, glaring mistrustfully at Raven.

With a huff, Herja took the blanket from her and strode forward. She draped it over Raven's shoulders. They were much thinner than Herja remembered; she remembered wrestling matches and constantly losing. If she and Raven ended up wrestling right now, Raven would lose for sure.

"It's true?" she prompted, kneeling beside her friend.

Raven nodded. "When I heard about it, I had to go. I was dreadfully unhappy and thought everything would be better if I could be a witch or dragon. I thought that something had gone wrong, that I was meant for better things than to be a human."

Herja touched Raven's shoulder, wanting to comfort them, but they shied back.

"Humans are vital to the health of Eldavon," Kaia said from where she stood near Nolen. "Without their Earth Magic—"

"Would you be so happy to be human yourself?" Raven asked bitterly. "Vital to Eldavon? Those words sound hollow when you can't do anything. When you're too sick even to walk, and you don't even have magic to serve the kingdom with. I wanted to do more and was stuck sitting by a window, darning socks.... I just wanted to be special."

"And what happened?" Herja asked.

"A man found me. He talked about the springs and said he knew where to find them. He promised they would cure me. So, I agreed to go."

Herja put her arm around Raven's shoulders again, and this time Raven leaned into her. They were thin and frail. It wasn't just the appearance from their wet clothes.

We need to build a fire, Herja thought. But even as she did so, there was a boom of thunder overhead, loud enough to make them all flinch.

Her throat constricted as she stared at the sky. We have to get back to the camp.

"We have to get moving," she said, urging Raven to their feet.

"The spring is real," Raven blurted, not moving. "But its magic is corrupt. It's something evil. It's turned me into a monster."

"A monster?" Penelope repeated.

Raven shuddered. "You have to leave me. Go to the spring and destroy it. Stop the man from drinking. You have to..."

They slumped forward with a groan.

"Who?" Herja pressed. Was it Finnegan? Was he back in their lives to torment them?

Raven shook their head. "You have to get to the spring. That's the most important thing. Herja—"

A loud huffing noise cut them off.

The hair on the back of Herja's neck prickled. She turned, holding her breath through some ancient instinct that told her to be utterly quiet.

A bear limped out of the forest. Blood matted its fur, and it panted. Herja could count its ribs. She slowly straightened, pulling Raven with her.

"Everyone, back away slowly," Penelope murmured. "Don't look in its eyes."

But it was too late.

The bear charged straight for them.

# CHAPTER

# TWELVE

KAIA STOOD FROZEN as the bear rushed at them, its paws thumping against the wet ground. Its jaws opened as it bellowed.

Hands grabbed her, pulling her out of the way. The bear's jaws snapped right where she had been seconds before. Kaia bit out a scream—how? It seemed like the bear had been so far away. She finally found her feet, fumbling backward as she reached into her pouch.

Spell. Magic. She whipped out her wand and pointed it at the bear. But before she could say anything, it had turned on Raven.

Raven fell backward as Herja was thrown in the opposite direction. The raggedy scarf that Raven held off their face slipped.

Danger.

It was like a voice spoke in Kaia's mind. She dropped her wand as she whirled, turning back to Nolen. He was already turning to help Raven. Kaia caught his face and pulled him away. He yelped, but Kaia only held him harder, knowing somewhere in the pit of her stomach that he couldn't look. That if his eyes turned back if he saw—

Everything went still and quiet. The bear's huffs were gone, and Kaia could barely hear the pounding of her own heart. She could only feel it hammering away at her ribs as she stared into Nolen's eyes, her hands cupped around his face still.

What happened? Kaia couldn't make herself look. A thick, bitter taste lay at the back of her throat, the sort of taste you get in the seconds before you vomit. She tried to swallow it, but it lingered there, nauseating her.

Nolen opened his mouth, then closed it again.

Slowly, Kaia lowered her hands. But she couldn't look. Something in her gut said something terrible had happened. If she didn't look, she wouldn't see what it was.

A thin, sobbing noise broke the silence and the spell of fear.

Kaia jerked herself around. She held her breath as her eyes skimmed over her friends. They were all here still. They stood in a semi-circle, staring forward with horrified expressions. The prickling at the back of Kaia's neck grew worse.

"We need to get back to camp," she insisted.

Raven was still on the ground. They pressed their hands over their face, the scarf back into place once more.

Kaia stepped forward but stopped. Nolen reached for her hand, staring behind her. His expression was just as horrified as everyone else's.

Reluctantly, Kaia turned.

The bear stood, poised to strike. Its mouth was gaping open while it lifted its paw into the air, claws stretched out for maximum damage. And it was also stone. Every hair stood out in vivid detail, its eyes frosted behind the glaze of rock, and Kaia could almost see saliva dripping from its gaping mouth.

Horror welled through her. She stood stock-still, trying to wrap her head around what she saw. It had been alive seconds ago. It had been attacking them.

Her hand reached out of its own accord, trembling as she stretched toward the bear.

Nolen grabbed her wrist and pulled her back. "No! We don't know if the spell is lingering still."

That bitter taste was back. Wickham's face had turned green, and he had both hands over his mouth. Penelope was half-shifted to her dragon form, her wings hanging loosely in the air. Kaia thought she had been turned into stone for half a terrifying second.

But no. That was just the turquoise blue of her dragon form, discolored by the stormy light they were bathed in.

Another burst of thunder broke overhead, but the storm seemed the least of their problems now.

Raven kneeled on the ground, struggling to tie the scarf into place. Now Kaia understood why they wore it, despite how difficult it must be to see and breathe in it, especially with it wet like that.

She stooped and picked up her wand but was still uncertain what to do. Her spells couldn't help the bear any more than she could help the deer.

Finally, Penelope spoke. Kaia turned to her, heart swelling with hope. If anyone knew what they needed to do now, it was Penelope. She'd be able to figure it out.

"We need to find shelter. It feels like the storm is coming back in," she said. "I can't fly in this sort of weather. Too windy."

She closed her eyes, and her wings retreated. Then she let out a shaky breath and turned to Wickham. "You've got twenty minutes to forage some herbs that we can use to help prevent Raven from getting sick. Herja, don't let him out of your sight."

Kaia cleared her throat, waiting for Penelope to give her orders.

"Nolen," Penelope said, turning to them, "I want you and Kaia to collect wood. One armful each will be fine. Nothing that we can't just snap off ourselves."

"What are you doing?" Raven asked. Their voice was hoarse.

"Taking care of the situation," Penelope replied. "We need to get you dried off and warmed up. Otherwise, you're going to catch your death of cold."

Raven let out a pitiful laugh despite the ragged sobs. "That should be the least of your concerns! You saw what just happened here. So you have to leave me. I'm dangerous. I'm a monster. If you stay, that will happen to you, too!"

Nolen put a protective arm around Kaia, drawing her back. She let out an annoyed huff, even though she appreciated his protectiveness. It was instinct for him after the way it was instinct for her to cheer people up when they were feeling down.

"Is it random, or only when your scarf falls?" Kaia asked, twisting her wand in her hands.

Raven remained as they were, but the sobs tapered a little. "When my face is revealed... anything that looks into my face turns into stone. I can't control it. I don't know what happened. Other than the Spring cursed me for my arrogance."

Kaia glanced over at Wickham. Their eyes met, and she bent one eyebrow upward.

Arrogance? She was curious to know if that was the word she would have chosen. Everyone wanted a purpose in life. She couldn't precisely say that if she was so sick, she could only darn socks. She'd be happy with her lot in life.

Wickham seemed to think along the same lines as she was. "You said that you could only sit by the window," he said, moving forward. "How did you get here? Were you getting better, or did the spring heal your sickness?"

"It destroyed me!" Raven tied their scarf tighter around their head. "It's a perversion of magic, and I never should have listened to him. But you can't let him get at it. Please! I'm a danger to you, and I'll take the consequences of my actions. Just leave me behind. It's better that way."

If Raven was even half as stubborn as Herja, how could the group convince them to come along?

Kaia's heart sank. They couldn't just leave Raven out here alone. If anyone could figure out what happened to them, it was Headmasters Twila and Valiant. If this magic only worked when something saw their face, they just had to keep it covered.

Kaia turned to Penelope, silently asking, what do we do?

Penelope stared up at the sky as though she had no answer. Kaia's hands clenched. What were they going to do?

WICKHAM STOOD NEAR HERJA, his hand resting gently on her arm. He wanted desperately to comfort her, but the rigid way she held herself told him she wouldn't accept it even if he tried. He should count himself lucky to have her let him touch her.

His heart ached for Raven. Regardless of why they went to this new magic spring, they didn't deserve it. He couldn't imagine the fear and guilt they must feel right now.

But if he was correct in his guess, the spring had strengthened them. With their thinness, they should be flat out with a fever after wandering around in soaking-wet clothes for who knows how long.

Instead, they got back to their feet and, while they shivered, showed no sign that it was anything more than a chill.

He glanced around, looking for any plants he could use to help any of them.

Raven's plight tugged at his heart, but it was also clear that whatever magic was on them, they were dangerous to him, Herja, and the others.

So, what were they supposed to do? They couldn't just abandon Raven, but at the same time, being around them was dangerous.

"The wind isn't as bad right now," Penelope said in her usual calm manner—Wickham felt a pang in his stomach.

No, he didn't want to be a leader like Penelope was, but he envied how she kept a level head despite these trying circumstances.

"I think we're going to have to risk the flight after all," Penelope continued. "The sooner we're back at camp, the sooner we'll have help to figure out what exactly to do with this new spring. We can't make that decision on our own, not when we don't know the full extent of the situation."

Raven stood facing the stone bear.

Wickham found a patch of moss. Not great for much, but if he dried it out, he could use it as a temporary bandage.

"We need more advanced magic users on the job," Penelope said, her voice firm. "So if we can get Raven back to camp—"

"I'm not going anywhere," Raven insisted.

Penelope tossed her red hair over her shoulder and glared at Raven's back. If Raven could see her, Wickham was sure they would reconsider.

"I'm too dangerous," Raven continued.

"Nonsense," Penelope said.

Raven pressed both hands over their face-scarf, hiding their face more firmly as they turned. "I am."

"Only if the scarf slips. So, Kaia, please put a spell on Raven's scarf to keep it in place. Then we don't have to worry about it slipping out of place. There. Danger over," Penelope said, putting her hands on her hips.

"I can do that," Kaia said, sounding relieved.

Penelope nodded. "Then that's settled. We'll use Herja's book bag; everyone can climb into it. The winds are gusting badly, but only after the thunder, so I'll have time to get to the ground whenever I hear it. So that's that."

"Bookbag?" Raven repeated.

Herja let out a soft little noise as though she was also relieved. Wickham tried to catch her eye, but she was staring at Raven still.

"I have a special bag that was given to me so I could carry all my books at a fraction of the weight," she explained to Raven. "But it's kind of changed purposes since then. It's big enough for us all to fit in."

Kaia approached Raven. Her wand was out. "May I?"

Raven hesitated but nodded.

Kaia pointed the wand to one side of Raven's face at the scarf. "Stay in place. Cover this face. Don't slip, even if Raven does a flip."

A warm light bathed Raven's head. Wickham got the sense of something lumpy under the hood they wore, but the light died down soon, and he was left with just the vaguest impression.

"All right, that's that then. Herja," Penelope turned to them. "Where's your bag?"

Herja turned. "I dropped it when the bear—"

She stopped.

Wickham turned, and the air left his lungs. Standing in the trees behind them was a man who was far too familiar. Herja's bookbag swung from one hand while he held a short sword in the other one.

"Well, well, well," Finnegan sneered. "Looks like I caught a bunch of little lost children in the woods."

# CHAPTER
# THIRTEEN

NOT THIS GUY AGAIN.

Herja's hands clenched into fists as she glared at Finnegan. It was bad enough that he had harassed them—again!—but that was her bookbag! If he wrecked it, she would be furious.

Almost as angry as she was right now. He must be the one who brought Raven up here on the mountain in the first place. He was the one that convinced her to drink from the spring. How had he even found it? Had he drunk from it already?

If he had, he didn't end up with the same sort of magic Raven did. Otherwise, they'd all be stone by now.

The thought cooled Herja's temper. Then she and the other two dragons stood before Raven and the witches. He might have a sword, but with their training, Herja was confident they'd be able to disarm him.

If he had an unknown magic? Not so much.

"I can't believe we're in this situation again," Kaia murmured.

Herja grunted her agreement. What was it with Finnegan that he kept cropping up in their lives like this? It was getting annoying... not that he wasn't dangerous, he was, but Herja had too much already in her brain to think too deeply about that.

"Now that I have your attention," Finnegan drawled.

Kaia interrupted. "Before we get to that—and yes, I know you want me to be silent—I have one question for you. One question, that's it. I'll stop talking."

Finnegan's nostrils flared as his eyes narrowed at her. Despite his obvious annoyance at her, he also leaned forward again as though he was interested in what she would ask. "What is it?"

"I'm just wondering if you were planning on returning to Odentia after all this is over." Kaia's tone was calmer than Herja expected.

Out of all of them, she was the one who had the most lingering fear of Finnegan.

He brandished his sword at her. "Of course, I'm going back! Now shut up. I'll cut your tongue out if I hear one more word from you."

A flickering heat built in Herja's chest, and she rolled to the balls of her feet. She might not have been able to protect the witches in the Silent Marshes two years ago, but she was faster, stronger, and older now.

Finnegan would not get away with threatening her friends anymore.

"Threaten her again," Nolen said challengingly. He bent his knees, ready to spring forward. His fingertips turned into claws, and it was as though smoke trailed from his nostrils. "Are you really willing to take on a dragon?"

Finnegan looked uncertain for a moment. His sword swung around to point at Nolen.

Penelope spoke dryly. "You may want to rescind your whole 'Kaia can't talk' thing. Nolen, here is her mate... do you know what that means? It means he will die to protect her. It also means she's the only one to tell him to stand down."

"You're not real dragons yet. I've been watching you. You can't shift forms," Finnegan sneered.

Herja folded her arms. "Maybe not all the way. But do we really need wings to burn you to a crisp?"

Nolen growled, and this time smoke did roll from his mouth.

Finnegan stared at him, uncertain.

"But you're right about one thing," Penelope interjected. "We don't like to resort to violence here in Eldavon. So, take back your threat to Kaia, let her reassure her mate, and we can discuss this. After all, I saved you from that kelpie two years ago. Do you really think swinging that sword around is necessary?"

The Odentia warrior gazed down at his sword, snorted, and lowered the point toward the ground. "Fine. I won't cut out any tongues. But you children are going to do what I want you to do."

Kaia tugged on Nolen's arm. "Let's hear him out; I'd rather not things turn nasty."

"Oddly reasonable of you," Finnegan sneered.

Kaia shrugged. "I guess I just don't understand why you would decide to escape from the Eldavon prison when you were in clearly better conditions, and now you're trying to go back to Odentia, where they treated you so poorly."

"That's true," Herja agreed with a nod. "I would like to know what your plan is. It doesn't seem logical, but I'm sure you've thought it through."

Raven hissed behind her. "What are you all doing? He's a madman, he's—"

"Finnegan," Wickham said. "The Odentian king's brother. I think, brother. Or was it nephew?"

"Brother," Finnegan grumbled.

Herja nodded. She remembered that much. "You're after the new springs, isn't that right? Because you can't get at the Silver Springs, not when it's so protected. So again, what's your plan?"

It was bizarre to Herja how the conversation had turned so... well, conversational. If anyone had ever told her she'd be in this situation, she would have assumed she was furious and terrified all at once, the way she was in the Swamp with the witches that she couldn't protect.

Now, however, it was like the scales of fear had been pulled off her eyes. Finnegan wasn't actually that much older than they were, maybe five or six years. He was an adult, but hints of childhood still lingered on his face.

A crack of thunder made her drop into a crouch, staring upward as panic shot through her. The possibility of more thunder was certainly more frightening to her than Finnegan with his sword.

"Let's get back to the cave," Penelope said, looking worriedly at her. "We can set up until the storm passes and discuss the situation at hand there. Plus, you look hungry; we can make some food and—"

"Quit trying to fool me with your fake niceties," Finnegan hissed. "I know you're just trying to trick me. I'm smarter than that! All of you are going to go into this bag," he shook the bookbag at them, "and then I will have my prisoners to negotiate passage out of this fake kingdom."

"Fake?" Herja repeated.

"Fake!"

"But we have kings and queens," Wickham protested. "How is it fake?"

Finnegan rolled his eyes. "Fake because you all pretend to be so concerned for each other. Nobody is this nice. You're all puppets and don't want to admit it."

Herja eyed the sky nervously. Being in the bookbag didn't sound like that bag, really... unless Finnegan intended to tie the end shut and toss them into a river. It wasn't exactly waterproof, after all.

No, she had to keep him talking so that someone would come up with a plan of how to disarm him. "Er, no, thank you. Let's go back to the cave."

"That's not a suggestion—"

"Is your plan to get magic and then return to Odentia and overthrow your brother?" Herja blurted.

Finnegan stared at her incredulously. "When I have magic and return to Odentia, my brother will welcome me with open arms. He'll forgive my past mistakes because I've brought him what he most wants. I'll be his right-hand man, and nobody will ever come between us again."

Herja was taken aback by Finnegan's response. She had assumed that Finnegan's goal was to claim the throne of Odentia for himself. He seemed too arrogant and ill-tempered to happily bow to another person.

But why did she assume that? Nothing he'd ever said showed that he had such lofty goals. Now that she thought about it, his actions, when she stepped away from how deeply personal they were to her and her friends, were really acts of desperation.

His words hinted at a deep desire for his brother's approval and acceptance. The tragedy of the situation struck Herja. Here was a man who would do anything, including steal magic, to win the love and respect of his own flesh and blood.

"I suppose I can understand," Herja murmured. "I'm an orphan, never had a family. But I think I would do whatever I could to win their affection if I had a family."

"That's not what family does," Kaia said.

Finnegan glared at her.

She lifted her chin stubbornly. "It's not. If you have to earn their love, then they're not family. Family loves you anyway. I think little of your brother if he makes you think you need magic to be worth anything."

"I agree," Wickham said, folding his arms. "I thought you were trying to be king of Odentia. But this? I'd never treat my brothers like that. I'd like to give your brother an earful—he's being completely selfish!"

Finnegan stared at them as though they had sprouted new heads.

A pang of sympathy hit her in the stomach. He was a man consumed by his own insecurities. She suddenly saw what Row did two years ago in the Silent Marshes. Finnegan might be a threat, but he was also just a boy. And not nearly as frightening and powerful as he would like to be.

"It doesn't matter," Nolen insisted. "It's not an excuse for the way he's acted. The way he treated Kaia and the witches in the Silent Marshes. Not an excuse for him harassing us again."

This brought Finnegan's sword back up. He pointed it at Nolen, grinning as though he just had his point proven to him.

"You're lucky I wasn't there when you were hunting the witches in the Silent Marshes," Nolen hissed, the cloud of smoke increasing around him.

"Nolen," Kaia said. "Stop."

"I would have let the kelpie keep you! You have no excuse for threatening innocent lives. You... you... villain!" Nolen shouted the insult.

A crack of thunder echoed him.

Herja gasped, flinching backward.

Finnegan gripped the sword tighter, taking her fear as a threat. "All of you just shut up! This is over—you're going to do as I say."

"Please, let's just get to the cave," Kaia begged. "Nolen, stop that. If we can just talk, we don't have to—"

"He tried to kill you once. I'm not letting him get near you again!"

Herja let out a shuddering breath. Let's just get out of this open space! She wanted to be in the cave or the cabins anywhere but here!

Penelope intervened, whispering to Nolen.

"We don't want to escalate the situation," she murmured. "Listen to your mate. Protecting her doesn't mean you have to immediately jump to violence."

"He has a sword," Nolen hissed back.

He did, but he was also incredibly scrawny. She knew from her research that he would have been well-fed in the Eldavon prison. So was his poor body condition leftover from his time imprisoned in Odentia, or was he sick, too? Had he failed to care for himself since escaping from the Eldavon prisons?

"Nolen," Herja said, but another crack of thunder burst out as she reached for him.

Screeches filled the air. Her head jerked up, and her hand clenched over Nolen's arm. Her nails dug into him, and she uttered a soft scream, unable to stop herself.

Nolen let out a roar, smoke bellowing from his mouth.

Finnegan roared in return, dashing forward, his sword above his head.

Kaia screamed.

Then a ball of fire at the space between the students and their attacker. Finnegan stumbled to a stop. Penelope pushed herself between him and the group in her dragon form. She stood tall and proud, flames licking around her mouth.

Finnegan took one look at her and booked it in the opposite direction.

Another massive screech above them was the sound of rock sheering apart.

"Stars help us," cried Raven. "It's the rocs—they've awoken!"

# CHAPTER
# FOURTEEN

WICKHAM GAZED in mingled horror and amazement as the rocs launched themselves into the sky from the distant mountain peaks. Lightning flickered through the air and arced between them. They looked the size of an eagle, but at that height... they must be massive.

He tried to think of what Herja had told him about rocs. Their wingspan was as large as a full-grown dragon. They could carry off horses and cattle without a problem if they fed on meat.

What did they feed on? He couldn't remember.

The rocs wheeled about, letting out those ear-splitting calls again. Wickham's heart slammed into his chest like a mouse caught in an eagle's gaze.

These were dangerous creatures. They were supposed to head down at once if they were caught on the mountains when the rocs came out. But they were also meant to stay in their tents.

His legs burned to run, but he couldn't make himself move. Not when the others were here, too, not when he didn't know if he should plaster himself to the side of the mountain or rush for the tree cover. Not when the massive birds both terrified and thrilled him all at once.

What would it be like to ride on their backs, he wondered.

Herja's hand wrapped around his. "Wickham!" she screamed right into his face.

Wickham turned to her, the mesmerizing spell breaking. Around them, the others were all staring up at the rocs as still as he had been. Was it magic? He shook himself and raced to Nolen and Kaia. He shook them.

Kaia jumped, yelping, and Nolen blinked rapidly like he wasn't entirely sure what was happening.

"Penelope," Herja was screaming now. "Penelope! Get back into your human form! Rocs are territorial. They'll think you're a threat if you get too close."

Penelope's elegant dragon form stayed as it was, staring upward.

Wickham let out a deep breath and raced forward. He braced himself for the impact as he smashed into Penelope's underbelly. The impact barely moved her, but it was enough to startle her from her reverie.

She retook her human form just as the rain came down.

It was as though they were suddenly standing in a waterfall. The force of the rain knocked Wickham off his feet. Herja pulled him back up. She took off her belt and his, then lashed them together. Everyone else offered their belts, and with that, they managed to make a rope.

Wickham didn't know how they would find shelter, but Raven took the lead. They led the group without faltering back to the cave where the students had taken refuge the previous night.

Without the bookbag and all the supplies they had in there, all they could do was to set up the blanket across the cave entrance to keep out the worst of the wind and rain. Herja and Wickham could change into dry clothes, while the others once more had toga blankets.

Wickham almost envied them. While he had a shirt and pants, they looked cozier in their blankets than he felt. He shivered terribly as he wrung his long silver hair out.

"Do we have any food left?" Nolen asked where he was spreading small, broken branches out to dry.

Their fire was tiny and pitiful, but they could not keep it going with how wet everything was.

"No," Penelope replied. She rubbed her forehead. "Finnegan took everything when he got his hands on the bookbag."

"How did you even drop it?" Kaia asked, turning to Herja.

She shook her head, scowling. "I don't really remember."

"But—" Kaia started.

Wickham waved his hand at her. "Does it matter? The point is that Finnegan has it now. So we'll have to wait until the storm is over, and then we will have to return to camp."

Silence met his words. When he looked up from the tiny fire to their three dragon companions to find them all looking at each other with weary expressions, his heart dropped.

"We need to get back to camp! We need the professors. You said so," he added, staring at Penelope pleadingly. "We can't take on Finnegan alone."

"I said we couldn't figure out Raven's problem alone," Penelope said slowly.

Kaia sighed. "But now you think Finnegan is another issue altogether, don't you?"

Wickham closed his eyes.

"We can't just let him wander around, and we certainly can't let him get to the springs. Raven is one thing, but we all know Finnegan will get the magic any way he can."

"But he was trying to take us prisoners," Wickham argued. "That means he'd rather have us as hostages than the magic."

Kaia made a noise of disagreement. "Or he planned on making us drink to see if it would do the same thing to us as it did to Raven. We can't underestimate him, Wick. Knowing it really is Finnegan changes things."

Did it really? Wickham wasn't sure why it had to. Was it because they knew him as a threat or because he was so desperate, he'd drink without caring about the potential consequences?

Wickham opened his eyes. He looked around at the group, but they all had determined expressions—except Raven, shrouded as they were.

"I guess there's nothing to it," Wickham said, defeated. "We'll have to get to the spring first and stop him from drinking."

HERJA CAME up with the idea that Penelope could use her flames to help dry off their clothes. The result had them all smelling like smoke, and poor Pen mushed in her dragon form, but it worked. Once they were all in dry clothes, they could use the blankets for warmth rather than modesty.

A good thing, too, because Penelope was exhausted from everything and fell asleep curled up with her back to the wall.

"You all get some sleep," Herja said as she settled in the space next to their barrier blanket, where she could look out into the storm. "I'll take first watch."

Kaia, Nolen, and Wickham found a spot on the floor and pulled their blankets around them.

Raven, however, finally no longer shivering, came to sit next to Herja.

And it was awkward. Herja did not know what to say. It had been so long since she'd last seen Raven and almost as long since they had last written.

"I drew a map." Raven handed her a piece of cloth, which had a crude map drawn on it with charcoal. "So that you and the others can find your way to the spring."

"I'm pretty sure it'll be easier if you lead us there," Herja said.

Raven shuddered and shook their head. "I can't. I tried to go back, but something was pushing me away. I think the spring is guarding against me. I'll lead you as far as I can, but... but now that you're here, and Penelope has an idea of how to help me... I think it might be best if I stay here."

"Here?" Herja pressed. "You mean in the cave?"

Raven nodded. "I'll take the watch and wake you when the storm ends. Then I'll sleep while you all take care of the spring and stop Finnegan."

Herja hesitated. It sounded acceptable... she was exhausted, after all.

"What about you?" she asked. "You must be exhausted from everything that's happened."

Raven shook their head. "Not exactly. I... don't think I need sleep anymore."

Herja frowned. That sounded... wrong. But she wasn't going to question Raven further. It was clear how they talked before; this happened to them had traumatized them. And if they were willing to take the watch while the others slept, it was only a good sign.

"When we get back and have time, we should talk," Herja told them. "We have an awful lot to discuss."

Raven nodded. "Sounds like a plan."

Herja smiled at them, though she knew her face would be just as hidden as Raven's because of the darkness. She joined the others and found a comfortable position.

She wasn't aware that she had fallen asleep until a clap of thunder woke her. She bolted upright, screaming as terror clawed at her.

Voices repeated her shout, but they were lost in the continuous crashing that made the cave shake. She had to get out of here! The ceiling was going to collapse; it was going to crush her to death—

The sound cut suddenly.

Herja shook hard and burrowed into Wickham's arms. He patted her back, murmuring soothing things to her. The tip of Kaia's wand was bright, lighting the space. Everyone crowded around, trying to offer Herja comfort—except one person.

"Raven," Herja blurted.

She pushed from Wickham and looked at the spoke where she had left her friend.

It was empty.

Raven was gone.

⊹≽ঌ⚬ও≼⊹

THE CHAOS from the storm slowly subsided. Herja stayed tucked into Wickham's side, clinging to him like she had been for the last half-hour. Kaia finished her spells, muffling the storm, and slumped to the floor, exhausted. She ached from head to toe.

"It's okay," she said, trying to reassure Herja all the same. "We're—"

"Raven," Herja said. It was the first thing she had said since waking them all screaming.

Kaia blinked, then glanced at her companions. With a sinking heart, she realized Raven was missing.

"Where are they?" Nolen asked. He strode to the blanket and peered out, squinting. "I don't see anything."

Kaia held her wand higher and cried out when she saw a strip of cloth where Raven had been earlier. She snatched it up and saw Raven had written clumsily on it with charcoal from the fire.

"I left a map with Herja," Kaia read aloud. "It will show you where to find the spring. But I know now that you won't leave me here like you should. I can't fight with you on it, but I am not going back. I'm sorry if this causes you distress, but I'll be fine living out my life with this curse. Don't try to find me. I'm leaving the mountains."

Herja's jaw dropped. "They left?"

"There's more," Kaia said, clearing her throat. "Herja, please don't be angry. I'm sorry I brought you into this. You've done more than I could have asked for, considering the way I used to treat you. I'm sorry. Raven."

"How did they use to treat you?" Wickham asked quietly.

Herja made a disbelieving noise.

But Penelope was already on the move. She checked the belt rope they'd used to come here, then wound a blanket into the waterproof bag and tucked it into her knapsack.

"You all stay here and make your way to the spring after the storm," Penelope ordered. "I'm going to find Raven."

Kaia lifted her wand as the barrier blanket flapped and buckled under the force of the wind. "It's too dark. Take my wand. It will light your way."

"No, you're going to need it in case Finnegan finds you," Penelope barked. "I'll be fine."

"You can't go out there by yourself," Nolen protested.

Herja jumped to her feet, shaking but with a fierce look. "I'll come with you."

"No," Penelope said again.

A crash of thunder bounced off the muffling spell Kaia had put up. It was still loud enough to make Herja flinch. Her determined expression faltered.

Penelope took a deep breath. "Nolen, you have to stay to watch out for Kaia. Herja, look out for Wickham."

"We can watch ourselves," Kaia protested, but it was weak.

"If I don't get back in time, it'll be up to your four to stop Finnegan," Penelope reminded them. "I'm going."

She headed for the entrance, but Kaia jumped forward. "Wait! Let me give you a spell."

Penelope hesitated, then nodded.

Kaia pointed her wand at Penelope, trying to find the words. "Find them," was all she could say. "Know where to look."

Light flared, then faded. And when it was gone, so was Penelope.

# CHAPTER
# FIFTEEN

THE ROCS DOVE and bobbed through the lightning. They seemed to play with it, catching it in their talons like an eagle caught fish. Penelope would have been humbled to witness such an awe-inspiring sight in any other circumstance.

Rain pelted her as she trudged through the forest, the wind slapping her breath from her every time the thunder boomed.

Despite the struggle to make headway, she pressed on. Her feet splashed through puddles; her clothes soaked through once more. Her red hair was brown with mud and grime from the many times she'd slipped on the steep mountainside. Red, bleeding rashes ran up both arms from where she'd fallen.

Her heart pounded in her chest, and her breathing came in gasps.

As she emerged from the trees, she saw Raven's silhouette, standing tall and still in the rain. Her hunch had paid off... this was the clearing where the bear had been turned to stone.

Raven stood next to the bear. Their hood had been thrown off, the scarf dangling in one hand as they stared at the sky. Rain fell around them, and Penelope was reminded suddenly of the old stories about gods and goddesses who had once walked the world before they left to give the first people space to learn and grow.

Lightning flashed. In that split second of illumination, she saw something like snakes writhing around Raven's head, like a living crown.

Then the thunder came, bringing with it darkness once more. Penelope shuddered as she forced herself forward.

She opened her mouth to call out but stopped herself. If Raven looked her way, she'd be turned into stone.

Unless... unless it was that whatever looked into Raven's face turned into stone? One of the old legends crept into her mind of a woman cursed to have snakes for hair and a gaze that turned anyone looking into her eyes into stone. She was said to be the mother of basilisks, who changed their victims into stone, but only if you looked into their eyes.

It was worth the chance.

Penelope covered her face, making her way into the clearing. "Raven," she shouted. "Raven, come back with us!"

A cry answered her. "No! Turn away, and you'll turn into stone!"

"I have my eyes covered," Penelope yelled, still inching forward. "Raven, listen to me. You need to look me in the eye to turn me into stone. I'm safe."

No answer.

"I'm going to lower my arm." Penelope took a deep breath. "Raven? If you don't answer me, I'll have to assume to run off—and I'll chase you."

"Don't," Raven yelled back.

"I will!"

"I'm telling you not to!"

"Too bad. I'm stubborn like that." Penelope lowered her arm.

A choking feeling seized her throat. For half a second, she panicked, thinking she was turning into stone. But the feeling passed quickly, and when her eyes adjusted, she realized that the rain had intensified even more.

Raven stood next to the bear, but their hood was up, and the soaking scarf wrapped around their face once more.

"Raven, come back," Penelope told them, reaching forward. "Take my hand. We have to go back."

Raven shook their head. "I can't. You know why. I'm getting sick and tired of telling you that it's too dangerous!"

"You know Herja, you know how stubborn she is," Penelope replied and then laughed. "We're all just as stubborn. How else do you think we make such good friends?"

"For your own sake and the sake of the others—"

Penelope shook her head, coming closer. "We're not leaving you. You're putting us in danger now, Raven, by running off like this. We can get you some help... you deserve to have help!"

Raven replied, but whatever they said was caught in a gust of wind. It blew Penelope off her feet, and she tumbled to the ground. Twigs and brush stabbed into her skin, and she rolled, grunting. Finally, she hit something that stopped her journey. The air was knocked out of her, and she sank several inches into the soupy, muddy pit.

What looked like a hand reached out to her in the darkness, and she took it, pulling herself up.

Lightning flashed.

And she stared into a face.

A scream burst from her instinctively. Monstrous fangs gaped in an open mouth toward her. Was this Raven? Was this why they said they became a monster?

Penelope braced herself, waiting to be turned into stone.

The lightning flashed again. In the illumination, she saw the creature was stone-grey. She grew aware that the 'hand' she held was stone cold. The bear had attacked them earlier, the one that Raven had turned into stone.

Penelope backed away, crawling through the mud to get away from it. She scrambled back to her feet, looking around wildly. Where was Raven? It was impossible to see with all of this rain!

"Raven?"

No answer.

Penelope clenched her fists tightly. She was shaking uncontrollably by this time, the freezing rain chilling her to the bone. If she took her dragon form, maybe it wouldn't be so cold... but then the rocs would come after her again, and this time she wouldn't have anyone to knock her out of the memorization.

Taking a deep breath, Penelope plunged into the forest again. The rain wasn't as heavy here, but the darkness was even deeper. She was forced to move slowly, feeling her way with her hands. Brush snagged her ankles and ripped her clothes, but she didn't stop.

Inside her, she felt a sharp tugging sensation, leading her which way to go. Kaia's spell. It was fortuitous that it hadn't broken yet—and Penelope shut down that thought, not wanting to test her luck.

Soon, she saw a figure moving ahead of her. They kept slipping on the ground, making their journey slower in their haste to pick up speed.

Penelope inhaled deeply and waited.

The thunder burst overhead.

A gust of wind smacked into her.

And in the few seconds afterward, there was stillness as the rain attempted to right itself again.

"Raven!"

The figure twisted, then started forward again.

Penelope hurried after them, clinging to the trees to keep herself upright.

Boom!

Whoosh!

Silence.

"Come back—we lost the map," she added, hoping the lie would turn Raven back.

No such luck.

Penelope pushed forward, following the brief glimpses of Raven's fleeing figure she saw through the trees in the flashes of lightning. The storm was growing worse than ever, and she stopped trying to shout. Her throat was raw already.

Both teens stumbled out of the forest onto the bald side of the mountain. From Penelope's angle, she could see Raven was headed straight for a cliff. Panic seized her chest as the rocs wheeled about overhead.

"Raven, stop!" she yelled, running forward. The grass was covered with a sheet of water, and she couldn't get a proper grip. "Raven! You're heading straight for a cliff! Stop!"

The horrible thought that Raven knew what they were heading for hit Penelope and made the panic surge even higher.

Raven's feet spiraled out from under them. They went sliding down the steep mountainside, and Penelope's heart stopped.

She threw herself forward, heedless of any danger. She tripped, slipped over the muddy, grassy terrain, and finally reached Raven, where she threw herself over the other figure. They slid, dipping from one side to the next.

They were nearly at the edge of the cliff before they finally came to a stop.

Both of them panted. Raven's hands dug into the dirt while Penelope braced her feet on a large rock beneath them. She wrapped her arms tightly around Raven and slowly helped them, likewise, to brace themself.

The water poured around them like they were lying in a shallow creek.

"No," Raven moaned. "No, you weren't supposed to follow."

"I told you I would," Penelope said. And despite the situation, she found a laugh in her voice. "That's one thing you'll learn about me. I don't give up easily."

Wait, why had she said that? Why would Raven need to learn anything about her? There was a good chance neither of them would make it out of this, and if Raven's stubbornness was any sign, they wouldn't have anything to do with Penelope once this was over.

"You're an idiot," Raven groaned. Their hands came to their face, making sure their scarf was in place.

Penelope shook her head. "I'm a dragon. My role is to protect others. And that includes you."

Raven shook their head. "But it shouldn't. Don't you see? I've been telling you—"

"You're not dangerous, you're scared, and something strange is happening. Just because you have dangerous powers now doesn't mean you have a dangerous personality."

Penelope wished Raven would leave it at that. It wasn't like this self-martyrdom was going to help anybody. They were so determined not to put others in danger, but Penelope thought it was more than that. It felt like they were punishing themselves to keep others safe.

"Don't you understand by now?" Raven demanded. They tried to wriggle free from Penelope, but she wouldn't let them. "I defied the sun and the moon. I spat in the face of their gift and decided it wasn't good enough. Whatever this magic is, it's not from the sun, moon, or earth."

Penelope pulled Raven in closer. "Since when do the sun, moon, earth, or stars punish us for our mistakes like this?"

"Maybe it isn't magic at all," Raven continued like they couldn't hear her. "Maybe I drank, and it stripped my earth magic from me. That's why I'm no longer human. Maybe that's why I'm not worth protecting anymore."

"Except you're forgetting something. Dragons and witches were created before humans," Penelope told them. "So, if you have had your earth magic stripped from you, you're one of the first people again— exactly who dragons like me were created to protect."

Raven grew still.

"You are worth protecting. The very fact that you are afraid of hurting others is proof of that," Penelope continued. "And think of it this way; you're not the only one. You found the spring because of rumors. Which means there are others out there, Raven. Others who have drunk. Aren't they worth protecting?"

"I..." Raven trailed off.

"Once we bring you back, once the adults figure out how to help you, then the others can know where to go. They can get help, too."

Raven trembled. "Do you really think so?"

"I do. We were brought here for a reason. Out of everyone in this world, it was you and Herja. Someone you knew you could reach out to. Do you think that's a coincidence?"

"No," Raven admitted.

Penelope pressed a hand to their back. "Then will you come back? Will you let us help you?"

Raven said something. But as they did, another gust of wind raced down the mountainside. A wave of water smashed into them. Penelope's feet slipped off the rock she braced herself against. Raven cried out. The two of them slid and washed down the cliff.

Then there was nothing beneath them.

They spiraled into the air, lightning, and thunder crashing through the air as the ground rushed up to greet them.

# CHAPTER
# SIXTEEN

THE STORM GREW EVEN WORSE once Penelope headed into it. Kaia stayed as long as she could near the entrance, but the backlash of wind and rain blowing in grew too much for her.

The four remaining students huddled together for warmth, but Kaia's hopes dwindled as the fire slowly burned out. Though Nolen encouraged her to rest, how could she? Penelope and Raven were out there in that gale, and she could do nothing about it.

"Why did Raven run away like that?" she finally asked aloud.

No answer from the others.

She sighed and tried not to overthink. This whole situation made her feel so tiny, so helpless. She had nothing to say to make herself or anyone else feel better.

When the storm passed, Kaia checked the blanket, which blocked the worst of it; and it was soaking wet. She didn't have the energy to use a spell to dry it off, either.

Every inch of her body ached, but with Raven and Penelope still missing, that was the least of her concerns. A headache pounded behind her eyes, making peering into the forest difficult. Everything reflected shades of brightness as the sun danced off the lingering waters.

"I think that storm was even worse than the first," Herja said. Dark circles smudged under her eyes, and she looked about ready to fall over.

That was a hopeful sign. Maybe Herja and Nolen would be too tired to argue about going for help.

"We should start looking for Penelope and Raven," she said. With the storm, she wasn't comfortable leaving them out here. "If we can't find any tracks in half an hour, we should head back to camp."

Nolen shook his head. To Kaia's surprise, he didn't look nearly as exhausted as the rest. But then, he was used to heavy rains and storms as part of the Swamp Watch.

"Penelope will either head to the springs or back to camp once she has Raven with her," he said. "We need to get to this second springs to ensure Finnegan doesn't get the magic. By this time, the professors will be looking for us, and we can set a signal fire once we're there so they can find us quickly."

Kaia's heart sank. They were really going to argue about this further, weren't they? "Nolen, I don't think I can keep going. I'm exhausted. I don't even think I could do a simple drying spell again."

Nolen's brows pinched together. "Would you and Wickham feel okay returning to camp by yourselves?"

"No," Wickham and Herja both said together.

"They're too exhausted to defend themselves if Finnegan goes after them," Herja said. "And there's a reason he confronted us rather than drinking from the Springs when he had the chance. I don't know the reason, but I'd rather not risk Wick and Kaia."

Nolen nodded. "Then we'll all have to stick together."

"Agreed," Herja said. She pointed up the mountain. "We go to the springs."

"No," Kaia protested.

Nolen took her hands in his. "I know that you're worried about Penelope and Raven—"

"Yes, I am." Kaia pulled her hands away from him. "And I'm tired of this argument. We've been trying it all on our own and have gotten nowhere. So why do you think it's a good idea to keep pushing and pushing and pushing when it's clear we're not getting anywhere?"

Herja made a disgruntled noise, but she paused as she opened her mouth. Then she cleared her throat and visibly bit back on whatever she had been planning to say. "I'm going to let Nolen handle this—my brain can't explain why."

Nolen gave her a 'thanks, I needed that' look, but soon grew serious again. "We need to put the good of the kingdom first. In this case, we need to get to the springs and guard it from Finnegan. Until now, we haven't had a clear destination or goal—now we do."

Herja nodded her support.

"Wick?" Kaia turned to the other witch, hoping that he'd have a better argument against it.

However, he had a troubled expression on his face. One that said he was still determined he could argue against Nolen's logic.

"The only thing is, what if they're hurt?" Wickham asked. He sounded like he might want to lie down right where they were and curl up to sleep. "Raven and Penelope could both be injured. They could have broken bones or be unconscious. If they are, with this weather? Even a few hours could be too late."

Kaia bit her lip as she searched the surrounding forest, hoping their missing comrades would just come striding out of the trees. It was a useless hope; she knew that, but it would solve a lot of problems.

"In that case, no matter what we do, it will be a mistake," Herja groaned. She pressed her fingertips to her temples. "All right. Here's an idea. Kaia, if Nolen and I took turns carrying you up the mountain, do you have enough for one more spell?"

Kaia flinched. Though both dragons were strong, she was sure she was too heavy for them to carry, especially on muddy ground. "I don't think—"

"Kaia." Nolen turned her to him, his steady silver eyes on her. "Please?"

She couldn't say no when he looked at her like that. Because she could see this wasn't about pride or thinking they could do something nobody else could.

No. Kaia saw the desperation in her mate's eyes. This was indeed what he thought they needed to do because if they didn't...?

She sighed heavily, not happy with the situation. "I might have the energy for one spell," she told Herja. "It depends on the spell."

"A knowledge spell," Herja said. "Cast on Wickham so he can know their state."

Kaia blinked. She'd never heard of such a spell before, but magic was unique to each wielder. Every witch had to create their own spell book for that reason. She considered for a moment, unsure. Would that take more energy than tracking them down?

If they carried her...

She sighed again and pulled out her wand. "I can try."

<hr />

WICKHAM MET KAIA'S EYES, trying to initiate some sort of mind-to-mind communication. It should help the spell move easier and take less energy from her. He waited patiently as she pointed her wand at him.

"Let him know the state that Penelope and Raven are in," she intoned seriously.

A flicker of light came from the point of her wind, momentarily blinding him. He winced and stepped back, shielding his eyes. But as he did so, a clear image came into his mind. Penelope was lying in a small hollow. Her red hair was pulled back, and a faint trickle of blood was dried on her forehead. But her eyes were open, and she was smiling as a mysterious figure rested their hand on her shoulder.

The image was gone.

Kaia ground and collapsed into Nolen. Her skin turned a faint greenish color.

Wickham dug into his hip pouch for some anti-nauseants and a precious few sugar cubes. Kaia needed energy, and fast. Usually, the sugar was used to help with other oral medications, to make them go down easier.

Wickham leaned back on his heels as they waited for Kaia to recover.

"I think they're okay," he admitted reluctantly. He had been hoping for an excuse to avoid climbing to the springs.

He was so exhausted that he did not know what the right choice was anymore. Face down Finnegan? Go for help? Find Penelope and Raven? Every option seemed like the wrong one for a host of reasons. He couldn't make this choice on his own.

He wanted to go to camp, find the professors, and give it to them. He didn't want this to be his problem anymore... he was good at healing. He wasn't good at guarding, searching or defending.

"What about the map?" Kaia murmured from where she was sitting. Her skin was losing its green hue, although there was no color in her cheeks.

"I memorized it," Herja said.

Wickham thought she sounded a little uncertain, but he trusted Herja's memory a lot. He rubbed his tired eyes, which was a mistake— it only made them more tired. He straightened as he nodded.

If Herja and Nolen thought their best plan was going to the spring and waiting there, then that was what they'd have to do. He rolled his shoulders, trying to lose the dull aches that twisted his muscles.

"Nolen, you look more rested; you should carry Kaia first," he said.

If they were going to do this, then they needed to get going right away.

"I'm too heavy," Kaia protested as she got to her feet.

"No, you're not." Nolen's expression and tone were both flat.

Wickham thought it was a bit harsh, but Kaia didn't react like she thought it was. She sighed and nodded once. Nolen crouched, letting her climb onto his back piggyback style.

They headed up the mountain, with Herja in the lead. Wickham came next, with Nolen and Kaia taking up the back. Despite being exhausted and hungry, Herja set a pace that Wickham struggled to keep up with.

After half an hour, they passed under a large rock, clinging to the edge, when laughter made them all jump. Kaia yelped, and Wickham turned to find Nolen had slipped off the path.

He leaped back and grabbed Nolen's arm... but it only dislodged his balance, too. The three of them tumbled down the sharp incline, falling in a bunch of bushes that tore at their clothes and poked their skin.

Herja was with them in a flash, helping them detangle themselves.

"Did I startle you?" a mocking voice asked.

Wickham looked up wearily. As expected, Finnegan stood on the edge of the rocky outcrop, grinning at them.

Only... he didn't look good. While they were all damp from moving through the forest, his clothes were plastered against him. Hadn't he taken refuge in Herja's bookbag? He was also using his sword to lean on rather than brandishing it as he had been before. And his shivers were unmistakable.

Wickham frowned, concerned despite himself.

"Looks like your friends have gone missing," Finnegan taunted. "That's too bad... maybe you'd like to reconsider your decision not to let me help you?"

Wickham frowned. When had Finnegan offered to help them?

Kaia got to her feet and helped Nolen up. Herja was already staring up at Finnegan with a fierce scowl on her face.

"Tell you what," Finnegan said as he lifted the bookbag in his free hand. "Why don't the four of you just climb into here? Get some food, dry off... oh, and do not try to fight me anymore."

"Why don't you just admit you're over your head?" Herja snarled.

Nolen nodded, glaring.

Wickham took a breath and a chance. He blurted, "I can treat that injury."

Both dragons looked startled, and Finnegan blinked a few times as he stared down at Wickham.

Beside him, Kaia shifted from foot to foot. "Finnegan—or is it Prince Finnegan?" she asked. "In the Silent Marshes, your men referred to you as Captain, but since the king is your brother...?"

"You can call me 'your highness,'" Finnegan sneered, but he still seemed off-balance.

Wickham internally grated at calling this man by such a title, but Finnegan seemed less well, aggressive toward them now. Was it because he was cold and injured or because he and Kaia were speaking more gently toward him?

"We can all go back to the cave," Wickham gestured. "You're soaked through and hurt. We can get a fire going so you can dry off and warm up. I have medicines that will help with the pain and to help prevent infection. Then we can all eat and discuss what we'll do next."

Herja hissed between her teeth. "What are you doing?"

"Trying something," Wickham replied.

Finnegan laughed suddenly. "Ha! You can't trick me that easily. I have the food. You have nothing. Pity—you should have taken my offer while you had the chance. I'm going to that spring, and I'll get magic more powerful than all of you. I'll turn you into stone!"

He took off, rushing up the mountain to disappear into the forest.

"Great," Herja growled. "We're going to have to move even faster now!"

As they went, Wickham couldn't help but wonder—if that was Finnegan's plan, why hadn't he done it already?

# CHAPTER
# SEVENTEEN

PENELOPE'S ARM and shoulder throbbed. It had been since she woke up, and it was getting to where she wasn't sure she'd ever feel better. Not that she knew how much time had passed.

On the other hand, only her arm and shoulder hurt. Badly, at least. Her head hurt a little if she moved her neck too fast. And in the shallow dip in the ground where she lay cradled her body so comfortably, she almost felt like she could fall asleep. Again.

"I told you to stay down," Raven scolded as Penelope started trying to push herself into an upright position.

The movement jarred her shoulder and made her whimper, but she got herself sitting. "I know, I know. But how long has it been daylight like this?"

Raven's shrouded face turned to the sky, which was bright and warm. "A few hours, I guess. You need more rest."

Penelope didn't dispute that; she needed more rest. Unfortunately, she didn't have time for more rest. She took a view of their surroundings. The previous night, she had been in too much pain to care about anything but getting out of the rain.

Now, she saw Raven had taken her to a shallow dip beneath the root systems of a giant tree. The way it was positioned on the hillside meant that the water from the storm flowed away from them while the sunlight was perfectly poised to filter between the roots.

"You really know this mountain, don't you?" Penelope asked, marveling. "How long have you been here?"

Raven hesitated before they shook their head. "I don't really know if I'm honest. I've lost track of all the days. I think it's been a couple of months, in any case. I thought if I stayed close by, I might be able to get back to the springs and drink again. Maybe if I did that, it would take the curse away."

"What do you mean by you 'might be able to'?" Penelope questioned, testing her shoulder.

Raven had built a small fire that warmed up the dip they were in. Penelope's clothes were still wet, but she wasn't too cold, given the fire. Her shoulder was still extremely stiff, though the slightest movement sent a piercing pain radiating through her chest.

Carefully, she used her other arm to fold the injured one into her chest, where she didn't have to hold the weight of her arm on her injured shoulder.

"Well?" she prompted.

Raven handed her a small pouch. "Eat these. The berries are for taste, and the roots to help with the pain. I'll also get a sling worked up here soon."

"Raven?"

Raven sighed. "I mean, I haven't found the courage to return."

Penelope nodded slowly. "I can understand that."

Raven made a disbelieving, snorting sound.

Penelope elected to ignore their disbelief and instead assessed her condition. After her shoulder, her damp clothing was the worst thing she had to deal with. There wouldn't be time to dry off before heading out again.

"I think you'll recover," Raven said as they fashioned a sling out of some old cloth. They tied it around Penelope's neck and carefully lifted her arm into it.

Penelope cried out as a bolt of pain shot through her. She closed her eyes and fought back the feeling that she was about to pass out. It took several moments for the feeling to pass, and when it did, she felt too sick to her stomach to eat the berries and roots Raven had offered.

"Try just a few of the berries first," Raven urged, pulling two tiny wild strawberries out of the pouch.

Penelope eyed it wearily, but opened her mouth. She was too scared of moving even her uninjured arm to take them.

The berries were sweet, and the brief explosion of flavor and moisture in her mouth helped Penelope to breathe through the last bits of pain. She risked lifting her uninjured arm, and though it pulled slightly on her wounded shoulder, it wasn't bad.

"I guess we're not going anywhere," Penelope moaned as she finished the few berries. She viewed the root with some trepidation, but if it helped... she chewed on it.

Raven leaned back on their heels. "You're an idiot; you know that?"

Penelope grunted in surprise at the bitter taste of the root.

"You shouldn't have gone after me in that storm. I know the mountain; I knew where I was going. You nearly got us both killed."

"If you didn't want anyone to come after you, you shouldn't have asked Herja for help," Penelope shot back.

Raven turned, grumbling. They added a few small branches to the fire and dug through a small pack Penelope hadn't seen before, but that made sense. For them to have been on the mountain for so long, they would have to have some supplies.

"That letter was for help with the new springs, not for me personally," Raven said over their shoulder. "I would have thought Herja would understand that."

Penelope frowned as she gingerly found a comfortable way to lean back, still sitting up. Raven had said something about Herja before. What had she meant by that? Would it be too much of an invasive question to ask?

The root, whatever it was, was helping. The thunderous throbbing in her shoulder diminished to a regular sort of throbbing. Penelope still didn't dare move it, fearing it would get bad again.

"Once you're able to move, I'll get you as far as the trail to your camp, but then you're on your own," Raven said, their voice brusque.

Despite the harsh tone, Penelope found she enjoyed the sound of their voice. It was melodic. "Why only that far?"

"Because you'll be able to get back to where you belong, and I'll go to find where I belong. There's got to be some way for me to make up for what I did."

Penelope sighed. So, they were still convinced that this was a curse... well, she couldn't blame them. To turn everything that looked into your face to stone? It was terrifying! Would it turn them into stone if they looked into a mirror?

Everything about this was unknown.

No amount of reassurance that the magics that Penelope knew would never torment someone like this would be comforting. If it wasn't punishment, what was it?

*Therefore, we need to get back because there has to be someone more qualified than two teenagers to fix this mess.*

But how was she supposed to convince Raven to do that?

"What I said during the storm still holds true," she said slowly. "Even though you're trying to pass this off as some self-sacrifice thing, it's not. You're not thinking about what's best for everyone else."

"Does that matter?"

"It does. How are you supposed to atone for your supposed mistakes by being selfish?"

Raven shook their head, their hood trembling in a way that Penelope was afraid would make it fall off.

"You and the others don't even know me. How is it selfish to try to protect you?"

"You're not thinking of the emotional impact," Penelope pointed out.

"But you don't know me. How can there be an emotional impact?" Raven sounded agitated.

Penelope wished she could see their face; what did they look like? What did their agitation look like? Was it stress, anger, or something else? "We're Herja's friends, too."

"*Too?*" Raven repeated. "What do you mean, too? I'm not Herja's friend—not when I'm why Herja was never adopted."

A TWIG CRACKED in the forest. Herja straightened from where she was crouched near the fire. Dusk was rapidly falling—they hadn't made very good time. It was driving her crazy, but she knew the witches were doing the best they could.

It didn't help that she wondered if they were making a mistake.

Now that feeling was even stronger.

Nolen came to stand next to her. Kaia and Wickham were busy cleaning up the roots and plants they had foraged for supper, commenting on how they were becoming real pros.

"It's Finnegan," Nolen said, scanning the forest. "He's tailing us. Keeps just back far enough that I can't get a clear look at him, but it has to be him."

Herja nodded once. "If he's following us, it means at least he hasn't gone to the springs yet. That's a good sign."

Nolen hummed. "Maybe it means he doesn't know where they are after all? Maybe he's hoping that we will lead him to them?"

"I don't think so. From what Raven told me, it sounds like they weren't strong enough to make it up the mountain on their own. Finnegan had to have taken them," Herja argued quietly.

"Unless Raven wasn't the only one who went."

Herja grimaced. She hadn't thought of that. But if Raven had had help other than Finnegan, why wouldn't they have told the group? It applied to the situation!

Nolen shrugged. "Or maybe he's waiting for the chance to take us prisoner, so he can barter out of Eldavon once he's gotten these powers."

"Or he wants to test them out on us." Herja pulled her fingers through her tangled hair. "In any case, we have to get to that spring before he does. We have to stop him."

WICKHAM SAT NEAR THE FIRE, watching their sad stew cook. The only good thing about being on these mountains was that they wouldn't run out of water. Food was hard to find, however.

"At least we found those dandelions," Kaia said aloud, as though she were reading Wickham's mind. She sat next to him and held her fingers to the flames. "Remember that weed stew that we ate in the Silent Marshes?"

Wickham made a face. "Ugh! That was awful. At least it was filling. But it wreaked havoc on my digestive system."

Kaia nodded. She glanced to where Herja lay on her back, then to where Nolen stood watching the forest. "If Penelope were here, she'd have been able to convince them to go back to camp for help."

"I'm not sure that's the best idea," Wickham admitted. "Nolen makes a lot of sense."

"If Finnegan were so determined to get to the springs and drink before we could stop him, he'd have done it already." Kaia lowered her voice, wrapping her arms around herself. "The more I think about it, the more I think this is a mistake."

Wickham shifted uncomfortably on the spot. "I'm not sure—"

"If we went back to camp, Herja could fly up here with Professor Delphine. Finnegan is obviously terrified of dragons." Kaia rubbed her eyes. "I'm just so tired, Wick. I don't think I can keep going. How can we guard against Finnegan if we're all exhausted and starved?"

Wickham let out a heavy breath. That was the problem, wasn't it? "I don't think there are any right answers... but the others will find us soon, Kaia."

He put a comforting arm around her shoulders. They would have help soon. The mountains weren't so huge that the other students and professors couldn't find them, even with the rain.

They would be found.

They'd have help soon.

Otherwise...

# CHAPTER
# EIGHTEEN

WICKHAM WASN'T ENTIRELY confident it was nighttime or just the warning of a new storm. His sense of time was all disoriented, but there was no thunder in the sky.

Which meant Herja was finally no longer so on edge. He'd offered to muffle the sounds for her over the day, but she refused, citing that he was already too tired. It was true, though Wickham wished he could help her more.

Kaia and Nolen slept first, while he and Herja took the first watch. It had been Kaia's idea so that they could have time with their mates.

Now, Wickham needed clarification on what he was meant to say.

"Herja?" he started awkwardly.

Herja rested her chin on her knees as she sat next to the fire, her eyes never ceasing their movement. She hummed in response to him.

"I was just thinking about when we went to the Silver Springs," he said as he took his hair from its braid. Twigs and thorns stuck in it, and he carefully picked them out. "Remember how you interrupted King Lantos to demand why we had to stay at the palace overnight instead of heading up Mount Eldavon immediately?"

"Yeah. I remember. I was impatient and thought I knew every-thing." Herja sighed as she shook her head. "What about it?"

Wickham chuckled. "Well, that was when I decided I would be your friend. After King Lantos talked to you, I thought you looked sad. I wanted to make you feel better."

Herja blinked as she turned to him. "You did?"

"Yeah. I'd never done anything like that, and even though I tried to tell myself it was for your sake, the truth of it is I wanted to be closer to you. I thought you were amazing and wanted to be more like you. You're brave and bold, and I admire that."

He picked up a twig and tossed it into the fire to have something to do with his hands.

When Herja didn't respond, he shrugged. "I'm not sure if my reluctance to go to the springs now is out of fear or if I really think it's better to return to camp. I don't know what my role as your mate is supposed to look like."

Herja's black brows furrowed over her silver eyes. "You being my mate doesn't make a difference in the best course of action."

"Maybe not, but it makes a difference to me. I don't know if I'm supposed to argue with you and somehow make the argument a respectful disagreement or if I'm supposed to shut my mouth and just do what you think is best. You're the dragon; you're the one who is supposed to be the protector. I'm supposed to be the healer."

Herja's arms fell to either side of her. Her back stiffened, and the look on her face made Wickham flinch.

"You're mad at me now," he stated dully.

"I'm not mad. I just... that's not how it works," she said, and although she said she wasn't mad... she sounded angry.

Wickham flinched again.

"Don't you remember what else we were taught on that journey?" she demanded. "Remember how we were told that while there were certain patterns that witches and dragons fall into, those weren't the only way? You're acting as though my being a protector and a healer are our only options. And it's not."

"But I am supposed to support you," Wickham protested weakly.

Herja shook her head, her glare icy. "Yeah, and I'm supposed to support you. This isn't a one-way street." She added another log to the fire. "This is exactly why I didn't want to have a fated mate. You should have been paired with Pen, not me."

Wickham's jaw dropped.

He had suspected that Herja was unhappy to have him as her fated mate, but for her to come right out and say it?

He dropped his chin to his chest, his shoulders hunching inward. What could he say about that? While he liked Penelope just fine as a friend, he couldn't imagine anything else between them. That he wanted a romantic relationship with his fated mate?

No, because that would only make a bad situation worse. To his embarrassment, tears burned his eyes.

But Herja wasn't done.

"I've always been better on my own," she said, glaring into the fire now. "I did my best to make sure I wouldn't have to rely on anyone. I know I'm no good at this sort of thing. What were the stars *thinking*?"

Wickham opened his mouth but couldn't speak around the lump in his throat.

"Penelope would know what to do," Herja continued, her voice lowering. "She'd know what it means to be a fated mate. I don't under-stand. I'm not...."

Wickham slowly looked up. He hoped that the tears wouldn't be apparent in the firelight. Sucking in a deep breath, he managed to ask, "Not what?"

Herja groaned as she rolled her head back, staring upward at the black sky. "I'm not good enough."

Wait, what? She couldn't mean that! Wickham sat back, shocked at what he was hearing. "What do you mean?"

"I mean, I've always thought I was better off on my own... but I'm not, and I don't know what I'm supposed to do anymore." Herja pressed her palms into her eyes.

"You don't have to know everything," Wickham said softly.

"I thought I wanted to be queen because I was so arrogant to think I could fix all the kingdom's problems. First, I was certain I wouldn't have a mate, and then I was convinced Icarus would be my mate. But you're my mate, and it's not fair to you," Herja said, her voice lowering. "It wouldn't have been fair to Icarus, either. I'm just not cut out for this."

"But you are," Wickham said, growing straighter.

To his surprise, he was *angry*. How could she think so little of herself? There was nobody else he'd rather be paired with! And she should know it.

"I would have been angry and disappointed if Penelope was my fated mate," he continued, not letting himself grow too shy to complete his thoughts. "Because you're my best friend."

Herja shook her head. "I know you wanted a fated mate you could fall in love with, though."

"I do love you."

Herja's shoulders drew back, stiffening.

Wickham bit his tongue. It was too much, wasn't it? He scrambled to find an excuse... but Herja operated best with the plain, honest truth. He scrubbed his face, his anger gone.

"I love you," he repeated. "You're my best friend. How could I not love you? Just like I love Kaia and Pen. But... but I do have romantic feelings for you, too, Herja. I didn't mean to tell you like this. But I hoped all last year that we'd be fated mates. Then when I saw your face after we were bonded...."

He shrugged helplessly.

Herja stared at the fire intently, her expression stern. Was she angry? Offended? Something else? She leaned away from him, and his heart dropped.

"I'm sorry. I never wanted to make my feelings your problem."

"My... problem?" she repeated, her voice stiff.

Wickham nodded, staring at the fire himself now. "It's not your job to pretend to make me feel better. I don't want you to feel like you're obligated to reciprocate. I know you don't feel the same way toward me, and that's fine. I just don't want to ruin our friendship."

HERJA CAREFULLY CONSIDERED Wickham's words. "So that's why you've been acting weird. Because you're trying not to force your feelings onto me."

Wickham blew out a heavy breath. "Yeah."

It explained a lot.

But knowing the explanation didn't help with Herja's feelings at the moment. What was she feeling? Was this relief or panic? Confusion or clarity? More importantly, what was she supposed to say? What was she supposed to do?

In the love stories she'd been reading, a moment like this would have her confess her feelings back to him.

What feelings were those, though? She wasn't sure what love was; how was she supposed to say 'I love you'? Those words should only be spoken when they mean something.

"If I've learned anything from my adoption records, it's that I have a history of pushing people away and not even realizing I'm doing it," she said aloud.

She wished they could stop talking about this, but then what? It wasn't as though Wickham's feelings would just shut off.

"I kept running away from potential adoptive parents, and now I'm suffering for it. I remember now how I used to think I didn't want to be adopted. But that was a lie because I didn't think I was adoptable. So, I made myself unadoptable and..." she shrugged, not even knowing where she was going with this.

"And now you feel like, since you weren't adopted, something is wrong with you," Wickham finished for her softly.

There was no judgment in his voice. That, more than anything, relieved the tension knotting Herja's shoulders.

"You're my best friend," Herja whispered, wishing her voice didn't tremble like it did. "But I don't think I can give you anything more than friendship."

Maybe, one day, she would be able to. But she couldn't give him that false hope. There were ways to break the bond between witch and dragon, and he could do that if he wanted more than what she could give him.

Wickham's silver eyebrows knit together as he worked his jaw. He was angry again. Herja resisted the urge to flinch. Of course he was angry... why shouldn't he be?

"That's exactly the problem," Wickham said.

"I know. That's why I said you should have—"

Wickham held his hands up. "No, wait, let me finish."

Herja huffed but fell silent.

"The problem is, a romantic relationship isn't 'more' than friendship," Wickham stated with such conviction it startled her. "Friendship isn't 'less' than romance. That's what I was trying to say. Because I don't want to lose you as a friend, I'd rather have you as a platonic fated mate than not have you as my fated mate at all."

"No."

Wickham rolled his eyes and let out an exaggerated sigh. "Yes. Unless you think you know me better than I know me... or you're calling me a liar."

He narrowed his eyes and bared his teeth at her, but she knew he was just playing. Relief washed over her. True, deep relief that made tears pool in her eyes.

"I didn't mean that," Wickham said, seeing her tears. "I was joking."

"I know." Herja scrubbed her tears away.

Wickham reached out his hand, offering it to her. "I value your friendship, Herja. I don't want my unrequited feelings to ruin that."

Herja nodded, accepting his hand. She made herself breathe normally, bringing her emotions under control.

Regardless of feelings, right now, they had a mission to accomplish. Maybe once it was over, she would have the space to think about Wickham's confession. Right now, though, it was enough to know that he valued her as a person and a friend.

"If Finnegan is still following us tomorrow, we might need to come up with a new plan," she told him. Maybe it was too abrupt of a change, but she felt like she needed a quick change. "We'll see what tomorrow brings. With any luck, the professors will find us soon."

Wickham nodded quietly. Herja was worried that she had offended him after all... but he didn't take his hand from hers.

And for now, that was enough.

# CHAPTER

# NINETEEN

PENELOPE CHEWED on another of the roots Raven gave to her as they moved through the forest. Raindrops glistened on the vibrant evergreens, making the mountainside look fresh and alive.

Luckily, after a full day of resting it, her shoulder no longer made her feel like she would die every time she moved it. Unluckily, it meant that she and Raven had been stuck, immobile, for a full day. She didn't like the idea of her friends facing down on their own like this.

"Are you sure this is a good idea?" Raven asked with a concerned glance at her—at least, Penelope assumed it was a concerned glance, as Raven's shrouded face twisted toward her. "I still think you should rest your shoulder more."

"Well, yeah, I should," Penelope replied, trying to grin. "But I can't."

Raven let out a noise that sounded like a scowl. "You yourself said that your professors and classmates will be looking for you all now. The mountains aren't that big; how long will it take for them to find us all?"

"I don't know, and that's the problem," Penelope replied. "The others will have either gone to camp or the springs. I assume they went to camp because the springs would be unguarded if they did. But like you said, the mountain isn't that big, and it will be found soon enough."

Raven nodded with a sigh.

The two continued. Penelope's injury slowed them down, but she pushed through the pain. Once this was over, she would probably need intensive physical therapy, but they had a mission to complete right now.

At least Raven seemed to take her words to heart. They weren't trying to run from her again, at least... although that was precisely what they had done before. Penelope wasn't sure if they had actually changed their mind or were just keeping close out of worry for her.

"I wish I could see your expression," she said in a sudden fit of frustration.

Raven stiffened.

"I'm having a hard time with being unable to read you," Penelope continued. "I—"

"You don't need to read me," Raven snapped. They came to a stop, their fists clenching.

Penelope stopped as well, her eyes widening. It's been an off hand thought, and she didn't think Raven would react so viscerally to it. "I only meant—"

"I don't care. You can't see my face. Stone, remember?"

Penelope flinched. "I'm sorry. I didn't mean to remind you—"

"Of course not." Raven threw their hands into the air. "This is exactly why I didn't want to be around people. If I have to live like this, I don't want to be reminded of it every time I turn around."

Penelope remained silent. Even though she wanted to reassure the other teen, she also knew it wouldn't do much good. Raven was going through grief right now, and no amount of reassurance would help them through it—this was too big a problem for Penelope to fix.

Kaia might know the right thing to say, but Penelope's emotional abilities were pretty limited.

"You don't have anything to say?" Raven demanded.

Penelope shook her head. "I don't think so. I've upset you, and I'm sorry about that, but other than saying sorry, there isn't anything I can say."

Raven's hands tightened, but they seemed at a loss for words.

"This is another reason you should come back with us to the Institute," Penelope continued, trying to keep her voice gentle. "You've been through something traumatic. It'd be good for help from professionals."

"Traumatic? What makes you think it's traumatic?" Raven blustered. "Even before the view of my face turned things into stone, I was hideous to look at. Now I have an excuse, and I don't have to listen to people lie and say I'm beautiful."

Penelope opened her mouth to snap back but swallowed it.

She knew what it was like to feel like she wasn't beautiful and to share those feelings, only to be told that she really was beautiful.

The first time she could remember feeling such a way was in their first year when she and the others attended the coronation ball of King Sydney and Queen Abigail. She'd watched Kaia dancing in her ruffled dress and felt a pang of yearning.

At the time, she had wondered what it was. Now, as she looked back at that moment, she understood it was because she looked so effortlessly happy and beautiful as she gazed at her friend. So feminine. Penelope never considered herself particularly masculine, but she also felt uncomfortable in the ribbons and ruffles that Kaia adored...

And part of her felt lesser for it. She wanted to be beautiful, even though she felt... shallow, somehow, for that desire. Whenever people complimented her looks, it was about her hair.

So, she knew what it felt like to long to be seen as beautiful by others... but not believe it when she was told she was beautiful.

Raven propped their hands on their hips, waiting.

"What do you want me to say?" Penelope asked her, shaking her head.

This all seemed like a trivial distraction when she knew Finnegan was on the mountain, creeping closer to these new magic springs—if he wasn't there already.

She had the sense that Raven was deliberately trying to drive her away.

"There's nothing to say, is there?" Raven replied. Their tone was bitter.

"Have you actually seen your face?" Penelope asked hesitantly. "After the change, I mean... how do you know you look any different?"

Raven seemed to deflate. "Only the ugliest of faces could turn another creature into stone. And how do I know if I look into a mirror, it won't turn me into stone, too? I don't want the last thing I see to be...."

They bent their head, and their shoulders shook.

Penelope nodded once. There was no use in pushing against this line of thinking, then. She started forward again, following the well-worn trail. It seemed the local wildlife reasonably often went to the new magical springs. Which begged the question, why would it transform Raven but not them?

Perhaps if she knew more about Raven's backstory, Penelope could figure it out.

"Are you okay with me asking questions about your illness, or do I need to talk about something else entirely?" Penelope asked.

Raven walked just behind her; their footsteps were silent. Eventually, they said, "You can ask. I don't know if I'll answer, though."

Fair enough. Penelope pondered the first question she wanted to ask. "What were you sick with?"

"Don't know."

Penelope started glancing over her shoulder, but pain sped down her arm and across her back, so she stopped. Instead, she breathed through it as she focused on putting one foot before the other.

Once the worst of it passed, Penelope asked, "You never got a diagnosis?"

"No. It was always one thing and then another... pain, coughing, weakness. Days turned to weeks and months and years." Raven's voice lowered. "But no answers. At first, the caretakers at the orphanage struggled to keep up with my needs... then I was adopted."

A mild edge came to their voice as they mentioned adoption. It reminded Penelope that Raven felt responsible for Herja not being adopted.

"Didn't you want to be adopted?" she asked carefully.

Raven was so quiet that after a few steps, Penelope had to turn to make sure they were still following. They were, although they had slowed down some.

Penelope shook her head. "You don't have to answer if I've over-stepped."

"No, it's fine. I wanted to be adopted. It was the happiest day of my life... but since then, I can't help but wonder if they only picked me because they felt sorry for me. Despite everything they tried, I just got worse and worse. There's no name for what I had other than a weak constitution."

"That must be so frustrating." Penelope couldn't imagine having so many problems with no answers. It made her feel sick to her stomach.

"It was—is," Raven said.

The two came through a few raspberry bushes, and Penelope had to stop. Her shoulder was throbbing again, and she carefully found a log to sit on.

Raven sat next to her and offered her another small piece of root. "Last year was the worst ever. I kept thinking that if this year was as bad as that, I'll never survive it. Then Finnegan came to my home, telling me about the springs. It seemed like the answer."

"Because you thought it would heal you?"

Raven nodded. "I thought, if I could just be a dragon, I wouldn't be sick anymore. Or if I were a witch, I would have the magic I needed to find my own answers."

And now they thought the stars were punishing them for wanting answers?

"At first, Finnegan frightened me. I tried to make him leave. Then he told me about his upbringing, about how his brother raised him... but always made him feel like a burden." Raven toed the ground. "I've always been a burden. Even when they told me I wasn't, I knew I was."

"And so, you were sympathetic with Finnegan, and he convinced you to come here?" Penelope pressed.

Raven nodded. "We rode his horse to the base of Thunder Ridge, then it got spooked, so he carried me up the mountain until we reached the spring. Then when we reached it, he told me to go ahead and drink. I did, and the worst storm whipped up... worse than anything since you've been here."

So, it was as Penelope thought. Finnegan had used Raven to test out the effects of the spring before he drank himself. Her hands clenched into fists, and she rubbed the knuckles of her free hand against her leg to hide it.

"Finnegan and I were separated. I spent the next few weeks wandering the mountain. Then he tracked me down. He was furious when he realized what happened, ranted that he hadn't gone through all this trouble just to end up a monster." Raven shuddered.

"So, he doesn't necessarily want to drink from the spring?" Penelope murmured. "Not this one, at least."

She thought about when Finnegan had confronted them after the bear attack. He'd been more interested in taking them prisoner than anything else... was that his game, then? Did he intend to capture them all and hold them as ransom to be allowed to drink from the Silver Springs?

It seemed to her that all the pieces were falling into place... and only made her heart sink more.

What could she, as a sixteen-year-old, do against him? He had been the one to take them prisoner on Mount Eldavon when they went to the Silver Springs. Then again, at the Silent Marshes, and now this. He was far more resourceful than they knew.

Was it wise to force a confrontation, especially now that she had more information about what he was after?

"I can't talk about this anymore," Raven whispered. "I can't...."

Penelope reached out and touched Raven's shoulder, wanting to be comforting.

Raven flinched at her touch, so Penelope withdrew.

"We should get moving again," she said as she got to her feet.

"Yeah," Raven said. They sounded utterly exhausted.

Both were quiet as they continued. Penelope knew they needed to be noisy, to let any wildlife realize they were coming, but she didn't have it in her to make conversation. The day dragged on until close to dusk when they made camp.

"I thought we would have found them by now," Penelope said as she settled beside the small fire.

"Maybe tomorrow," Raven sighed. They laid down and rested their head on their arms. "Something strange is happening here. Magic seemed to be out of sync. Something..."

They trailed off. Penelope shivered, and not just from the cold. She closed her eyes and tried to sleep. She'd deal with tomorrow and everything it brought when it came.

# CHAPTER
# TWENTY

NO WORDS COULD DESCRIBE Kaia's relief when Penelope and Raven finally caught up to the others.

It was the third day after the storm, and even though she could look down the mountain and see the rocky valley where the camp was, it felt as though they had made no progress. So, when Penelope's clear, familiar voice called out, announcing her presence, Kaia nearly broke into tears.

"Careful of my shoulder," she warned as Kaia came to hug her.

Kaia eyed her arm warily. It was in a sling, but the visible skin was all shades of black and purple. She flinched as she looked at it.

"I have a healing poultice left," Wickham said, immediately digging into the pouch at his side. "That does it; we have to get back to camp."

Nolen stepped up beside Kaia. "We've discussed this."

"We have," Kaia said, turning to him. "But that's all we've done. Discuss it and then continue."

Nolen's brows furrowed. "I'm missing something, aren't I?"

Herja and Wickham helped Penelope sit, and Herja helped Wickham tend to her injured shoulder while Raven stood by. Even without seeing their face, the awkwardness rolled off them.

"We've been coming at this the wrong way," Kaia said with a shake.

"It's seemed like a clear divide, dragons vs witches. But we haven't resolved it the way we should. We've been running on fear, and empty stomachs like we witches did in the Silent Marshes when Finnegan came after us."

Wickham, who was frowning at Penelope's shoulder uneasily, looked up. "We had a vote. But here, on the mountain, Kaia and I have let the dragons make all the choices."

"And that's not right," Herja said with a quick shake of her head. "We're meant to make decisions together... I'm sorry. I didn't realize how much Nolen and I were bulldozing through everything."

"And I didn't realize how much Kaia and I were making the decisions about your problem rather than helping to solve them," Wickham replied as he sat back on his haunches.

Nolen ran a hand through his pale hair. "I still think we need to guard this new spring against Finnegan. If he drinks from it...."

"He's had the opportunity, though," Raven said, speaking for the first time. They seemed to tremble in their shroud and hooded cloak, but their shoulders were straight. "We've been here for months now, the two of us."

Kaia frowned. This changed things. "And he's had the chance to drink?"

"I have to assume so. He's been chasing me, trying to convince me to return to his kingdom with him as his weapon." Raven took an audible breath. "Penelope has a theory that I think is quite reasonable."

One glance at Penelope, though, told Kaia that she wouldn't be telling them what it was. Her face had turned white from something Wickham had done. Her eyes were screwed shut, and she was visibly fighting back the urge to vomit.

Kaia hurried over. "What's wrong?"

"We fell over a cliff," Penelope said through gritted teeth. "Hurt my shoulder."

"Broke your shoulder more like," Wickham replied.

Penelope made a gagging noise, then swallowed. "Raven's got a root that helps with the pain."

Raven shook their head. "I'm out."

"What is it?" Kaia asked, turning to them. "We can find more."

"I... I'm not sure. I found it at the monster springs."

Herja looked up at the mountain. "So if we get there, we can get more painkillers."

Kaia nodded. "Yes, or we could find Professor Gable, and he could use his magic to help Penelope. For all we know, Finnegan is planning to force us to drink from the spring to see if it has the same effects as it had on Raven."

She gestured to the other teen, who flinched. Kaia bit her lip, hoping she hadn't offended them.

Penelope opened her mouth, groaned and leaned back against Wickham, now looking slightly green. Wickham had one hand just over Penelope's shoulder, but Kaia wasn't sure what he was doing.

"He can't force us to drink," Herja argued.

Wickham looked up here. "If Finnegan held a knife to your throat —any of you—I'd do it."

Herja opened her mouth and closed it again.

"Um, but here's the thing," Raven said, sounding nervous. "Penelope's idea. She thinks maybe Finnegan plans to take you all prisoner and then use you as hostages to allow the kings and queens to let him drink from the Silver Springs."

"Is that right?" Nolen asked Penelope, who managed a nod.

She really didn't look good. Kaia hurried over with her waterskin and crouched near them. "Wick, do you think I should try a pain-relief spell?"

"In your condition?" Wickham shook his head. "You know that those take a lot of you. And it'd take a lot of out of Pen, too. Maybe too much. There's a lot of damage here."

Herja straightened and looked up at the mountain, then back down. "We should have been making better time than we have had. The others should have found us by now; the mountain itself is possibly fighting against us going to the spring."

"I still say we go to it and guard it," Nolen said stubbornly. "If Finnegan plans to kidnap us, he might abandon it as soon as we're with the others. He might be desperate enough to just drink from this spring."

"If he can get to it," Kaia said. "The mountain's been fighting us."

"*Maybe*," Nolen corrected.

Kaia chewed her lip, nodding. There were many things to consider here. "So let's vote on it. I say we go back to camp. Who agrees with me?"

"I do," Wickham said, sounding distracted.

Kaia nodded again.

Nolen pinched the bridge of his nose. "I vote we go to the springs. Anyone else?"

"I vote the same," Herja said. "I can't accept leaving it unguarded."

Kaia blew out her breath. "So that leaves Pen and Raven."

"Me?" Raven sounded shocked.

"You're here," Herja replied. "You're part of this. You have the right to vote on where we go."

Raven was quiet for a long moment. "No. No, I don't think I do. I'm not going to vote."

Which meant... the swing vote was Penelope. Kaia turned to her. She was in such rough shape; how would she go up or down on her own power? Everyone was quiet as they waited for Penelope's decision.

⁘

PENELOPE COULD HARDLY THINK STRAIGHT, but she still felt the weight and expectations of her friends on her.

What was the right choice here? And why did she have to be the one who made it? She pinched her eyes shut tighter. It was true. She, more than anyone else, ended up as a leader in their small group, something that she never really considered until recently.

But what gave her more qualifications than anyone else?

"I don't want to make the choice," she groaned. "I want someone else to choose."

"I'm sorry. But we're at a draw. We need the swing vote," said Kaia.

A brief welling of panic went through her. This wasn't what she wanted. She never wanted to be the person whose choice affected others this way. And yet, she found herself in that position more and more often.

First, when she decided she would join the military. It greatly affected her family, and she hadn't even joined yet. And now this...

"Pen?" Herja's voice was soft, closer to her.

Penelope opened her eyes.

"It's okay if you don't want to make this choice right now," Herja said. "It's been thundering all day. We can find a place to stay for the night, get some sleep, and revisit the choice in the morning."

Penelope sighed. "No. I've already made my choice... I just wish it didn't come down to me because I'm not sure it's the right one."

She opened her eyes again, trying to keep her shoulder still. Whatever Wickham had done helped with the worst of the pain, but she could feel it hovering there, waiting to strike again.

As much as she would like to have another night's sleep without further moving, sitting still wouldn't help anyone.

"Are you sure?" Kaia asked.

Penelope gave her a strained smile. "We need to stop Finnegan, but we're kids. We don't have full training; we can't just go up against an Odentian warrior. I hate to leave Herja's bookbag in his hands—"

"That's the least of our problems," Herja murmured.

"But we have to get back to camp. If I take my dragon form, I can carry the rest of you down," Penelope continued.

Hopefully, in her dragon form, she could easily navigate this terrain. The only problem was the rocs, but with their penchant for thunder, she could always count on Herja to break them out of any roc-induced trances.

"Are you sure you can?" Nolen asked as he crouched near them. He frowned at the terrible bruises on her shoulder.

Penelope glanced at her injury. No, she wasn't sure at all. But they needed to move faster than they could on foot.

"If you push yourself too much, you could end up permanently damaged," Wickham warned.

"We can walk," Kaia added.

Penelope inhaled deeply, steeling herself as she pulled herself back to her feet. The pain was blinding, but if she tried hard enough, she could hide just how bad she was. Once she was in her dragon form, they could even tie blankets to the spikes on her back, letting her drag them behind her.

She didn't have to use this arm.

"We're going back down anyway," Herja said. "That's the vote. So let's try it with Pen carrying us down. If it doesn't work, then we can go on foot. Agreed?"

Wickham grunted. "Not really, but I don't have a better idea. I'm tired of the arguing."

They all were. Penelope straightened and reached inside for that fire she knew was there. Warmth spread through her, and she went to embrace the dragon—

But nothing happened.

The flicker that came to her so quickly stayed out of reach. She frowned, fighting back in an instant wave of panic. There was no need to panic. She was just trying too hard. All she had to do was loosen her expectations. Close her eyes and...

Nothing.

"Pen?" Herja asked softly.

She opened her eyes again and shook her head, fighting back tears. "I can't."

"It's your injury," Wickham said.

But was it? Penelope had never known injuries to prevent a dragon from shifting. She tried not to let her worries show—that was the price of everyone looking to you for answers. You had to have them. Or at least not show your fears.

Herja spoke up, sounding confident. "We'll get to shelter for tonight and head out tomorrow on foot. I know we're all tired and hungry. Maybe a good night's sleep is exactly what we need."

She shouldered her pack and smiled at them all.

Slowly, everyone else gathered their things.

"Nolen, what's that song you said you sing on your treks?" Herja asked. "Some music will lift our spirits."

"Yes," Kaia agreed.

Nolen seemed begrudging but started to sing. Kaia gestured for Raven to join them, smiling. Good—Raven needed to be integrated into the group. And Penelope didn't have it in her to keep her spirits up, let alone anyone else.

She couldn't shift. Was it the magic of the mountain?

Or something even more sinister?

# CHAPTER

# TWENTY-ONE

WICKHAM GROANED as he saw the inky black clouds gathering again. They didn't call these the Storm Mountains for nothing, nor was this particular mountain misnamed 'Thunder Ridge.' He just wanted enough time to dry off and stay dry for a few hours.

"We should get some shelter," Penelope said. Her usually tanned tones were a sickly green again—she needed a proper doctor.

What sort of damage was she doing to herself by pushing on? He didn't like to think of it. But at least they were headed back to camp, right?

"This way," Raven gestured. "There's a little cave a few hundred meters away; it should be big enough for us all."

The little group followed their shrouded guide. The wind picked up, bringing with it spitting rain. Wickham shuddered, looking forward to getting out of the elements.

But when they got to the cave and crowded in, they were welcomed by an unwanted surprise.

"Well, well, well," Finnegan sneered. "Look what—"

Thunder boomed. Herja screamed and clung to Wickham as the mountain shook. Wickham put his hands over her ears, wishing he could do more. The heavens opened, releasing what seemed to be a full-out waterfall dumping on the mountainside. Even as he watched, several small trees were uprooted by the torrent.

Surely these were unnatural storms they'd faced this past... week, was it? He had to admit; he'd lost track of time.

Nolen swung his pack off, reaching inside for the blanket they used to block the other cave entrance, but Finnegan stepped forward and placed the tip of his sword on the dragon's shoulder.

"Stop being dramatic," Kaia snapped at Finnegan. "We just want to block out the storm. Here, you can threaten me to keep everyone else behaving."

"Kaia!" Wickham yelped, startled.

Finnegan gave her the same startled look. He looked rested, dry, and like he'd had a good meal since the last time they'd seen him. His brows pinched together, but he snorted and moved the tip of his sword to Kaia's neck.

She looked... calm. Nolen growled, and everyone else tensed, but Kaia didn't so much as flinch.

Wickham's hands were still over Herja's ears. She stepped away from him, her eyes on Kaia and Finnegan.

"Nolen, put up the blanket," she ordered. "Between the sword and storm, I think Prince Finnegan is the lesser threat now."

Finnegan stood a little straighter to be referred to as a prince. Wickham wasn't sure how he was supposed to react to this. It seemed insane that Kaia was talking this way.

But it seemed to work. While Finnegan usually glared at her as though he wanted to kill her, now his gaze was more... smug? Wickham didn't like it, but as Nolen and Herja put up the blanket, Wickham had to admit that she was right.

Finnegan had tried to kill her in the Silent Marshes, and Icarus still bore the scar from the attack. This time, however, Finnegan seemed oddly reluctant to do any actual damage to them. He wanted them—all of them—for some reason.

Was it so he could turn them into stone once he got his new powers? Or to bargain a deal to drink from the Silver Springs?

Once the blanket was up, holding back at least part of the storm,

Finnegan picked up Herja's bookbag. "All of you will get into this now —except the redhead. You, Miss Dragon, are going to fly me to the springs as soon as the storm is over."

"Which ones?" Herja asked.

Finnegan shot her a glare.

"I can't," Penelope said.

Finnegan's lips peeled back, and Wickham warily eyes the sword at Kaia's neck.

"I broke my shoulder, and I can't shift into my dragon form," Penelope explained.

"Don't lie to me. I know physical ailments don't affect your ability to change," Finnegan said.

"I'm not—" Penelope started.

The sword on Kaia's neck moved closer to her throat, and Wickham blurted out, "Let's just get into the bag. We can all go in, and Pen can explain what happened after, right?"

He looked at his friends, trying to nod toward the sword as he did so. There was no point in getting Finnegan angry, not right now. They outnumbered him, yes, but he was armed and willing to kill, something they weren't.

"I disagree," Herja said, frowning at Wickham. "We shouldn't—"

"Herja." Kaia took the bookbag carefully from Finnegan and held it out. "Let's just de-escalate the situation, okay?"

Herja narrowed her eyes but took the bag. She set it down and crawled inside.

Finnegan's eyes darted to Raven. "You next."

Raven went in, keeping one hand on their shroud. Nolen went in next, but Wickham refused to enter until Kaia was, so he came last, and Finnegan tied the drawstring tight behind him.

While big enough for Herja to take some well-needed respite at the Institute or carry the supplies they needed for a few days, the bookbag was too small for five people. They had to sit with their legs cramped against their chests amid the barrels of supplies.

Or rather, empty barrels.

"Here's something," Nolen said after searching through the barrels. He placed it in the middle of the space.

The barrel was filled with nuts. Wickham didn't particularly like them, but with his stomach growling, he would not complain.

"Finnegan certainly went through a lot of food," Kaia said.

Herja shrugged. "I only packed enough for a couple of days for only a few people. So not really. It just seems like a lot because we're packed in here like sardines."

"Be quiet in there," Finnegan yelled from outside the bag.

They all glanced at the entrance and were quiet. Wickham strained his ears. It was muffled, but Penelope calmly explained how she had attempted to take her dragon form earlier in the day and was unsuccessful.

"Do you really think we would have been walking back down the mountain if I could have carried everyone as a dragon?" she asked.

Finnegan didn't reply, and the conversation fell silent.

"I'm sorry," Nolen whispered to Kaia. "I didn't mean to get you into this mess."

Kaia sighed. "Nolen, I'm the one that got you into this mess. Just because you're a dragon doesn't mean everything is on you."

Nolen frowned.

"For what it's worth," Kaia continued, keeping her voice low, "I feel much more confident and braver than I have before while facing Finnegan. Although I'm not sure I feel any smarter... I'm not sure how far he'd let me push him."

"That's a good point," Wickham said.

Herja nodded. "So, it's probably best that in the future, you stay quiet. He has proven to have pent-up aggression toward you. I don't want that to snap and for him to decide to make an example out of you."

Kaia let out a shaky breath. "Yeah. That's probably best."

Wickham's leg was cramping up, and he tried to adjust his position to straighten it out without bumping into anyone else. "We'll have to figure out a way to stretch out. This isn't good for our bodies."

Nobody answered because how could they? There wasn't room to stretch out. So Wickham rested his chin on his knee and tried not to think too hard.

THE THUNDER continually boomed from outside of the book bag. It took all of Herja's energy to keep still. She desperately wanted Wickham to sing to her again like he had the first night the others had found her. It felt wrong to ask for comfort, though, when Penelope still had to deal with Finnegan.

"I'm in pain," she said, her voice stressed. "I just want to get some sleep. Is that so bad?"

"Don't think I'm going to let down my guard and allow your little friends to escape," Finnegan shot back.

Penelope let out an audible groan. "I wouldn't dream of it. Now can I please shut my eyes and try to rest?"

Finnegan grunted, presumably allowing the go-ahead as they both fell silent.

Herja hugged her knees tighter to her chest. Bad enough that they were in this position at all, but to be tucked into a tiny space like this? The thunder only made it worse as her armpits dampened. Kaia and Nolen were murmuring gently to each other. On Herja's one side Wickham kept listening outside the bag while Raven sat silently on her other side.

A crack of thunder made Herja gasp aloud. She ground her teeth —they were prisoners, and she was still worried about a bit of thunder?

"I can muffle the entrance," Kaia offered, her eyes on Herja.

Heat rushed to her cheeks, and she shook her head. "No. Pen might need our help."

Kaia nodded.

They all fell silent. There was still no sound from Finnegan and Penelope—Herja imagined he was allowing Penelope to rest. She wouldn't be much of a threat to him with her broken shoulder.

Although how she could rest when that thunder wouldn't shut up, Herja didn't know.

"We shouldn't have done this," Herja murmured. She tucked her forehead against her knees to muffle her words. They didn't want Finnegan to hear their conversation. "We shouldn't have surrendered like this. We could have taken him."

"Not with his sword at Kaia's neck," Nolen argued.

Herja shook her head. "But all we really had to do was to threaten to have Raven remove their face veil if he hurt any of us. Simple. We should have done that."

"I don't think Finnegan is one to respond to threats, though," Kaia replied softly. "He's too used to them."

"How would you know?" Herja snapped.

Wickham nudged her arm. "Hey. We're going to be okay."

All her muscles felt like they were shrinking. She needed to stretch, to move. But the thunder kept booming, and the space kept getting hotter and smaller. She screwed her eyes shut, covering her ears. It wasn't okay. It would never be okay.

"Herja, it's going to be okay," Wickham repeated, putting an arm around her.

And even though she wanted the comfort, yearned for it, she suddenly couldn't stand being touched. She shied back against him only to hit Raven.

Too close.

Not enough room.

"This is going to wreck our learning curve completely," she burst out.

She knew it wasn't relevant, but having something to complain about made her feel oddly better. Her shoulders remained tight, and her lungs didn't seem like they fully expanded, but as long as she was talking, it didn't hurt so bad.

"Every year, it's one thing after another," she ranted. "My ability to learn has been severely stunted. That's why none of us can turn into dragons. It's always something happening, and how are we supposed to learn anything in these conditions?"

She didn't have to lift her head to know everyone was giving her incredulous stares.

"Herja—" Wickham started, his tone placating.

"How are we meant to plan for the future when we're constantly barely surviving the present?" Herja demanded.

She finally looked up and glared at him. Maybe that was why she both wanted comfort but couldn't stand it. It just didn't feel real... and they still didn't really know what Finnegan was after. This was the third time he'd targeted them. They were sixteen now, practically adults—who was to say that he wouldn't see them as threats to be put down now?

Kaia spoke up. "If we move all the barrels to this side, it'll make enough room for one person to lie on top of them and stretch out. Then, the other four can sit against the other wall and stretch their legs out."

Herja bit her lip, distracted from her anxious, running thoughts.

Nolen grunted and shifted the barrels around, moving them to one side. It wouldn't be comfortable, but it would work. They piled the blankets atop next to give a little cushioning.

"Raven, why don't you lie down first?" Kaia urged once they had it in order. "Your head keeps drooping—I bet you're exhausted."

Raven silently crawled atop the barrels.

It gave little more room, but if Herja sat facing the others down at Raven's feet, her legs stretched to the wall, at least she could breathe.

"I'm sorry," she said miserably, aware that her lashing out had only worsened things.

"Let's just try to rest," Kaia urged. "We can't think clearly when we're tired."

Herja leaned her head back on the barrels, closing her eyes. The thunder kept going, but it didn't seem as bad now. Kaia had made an intelligent move. Now... now they only had to wait to see what would happen next.

# CHAPTER
# TWENTY-TWO

DESPITE THE CHILL in the air, Penelope felt a little warm throughout the storm. It was a worrying sign—had her injury gotten infected? Her shoulder was even more swollen and painful than ever, so much so that she hardly felt like she could walk when Finnegan woke her up.

"Morning, little dragon," he said in a sickly-sweet tone. "Ready to head to the springs?"

His cheeks were a little pink, and it took a moment for Penelope to realize that the dampness clinging to his hair was due to sweat rather than the rain.

Penelope slowly got to her feet. She had done her best to wrap up her shoulder and arm so it wouldn't accidentally jostle the previous night. This morning it felt as though the whole side of her body was stiff, even down to her ankle. She wasn't sure how she was meant to walk properly.

"Are you still going to try to tell me you can't change into a dragon?" Finnegan asked her.

"I can't," Penelope mumbled.

Finnegan snorted. "Guess you'll have to pull your weight a different way, then."

He picked up the book bag, and Penelope eyed it. If she could get her hands on the bag, maybe she could make a break for it. Circumstances had forced them into the same space as Finnegan, but if she could get away...

"I'll carry the bag, then?" she said, trying to keep the hope from her voice.

Finnegan rolled his eyes. Thank goodness he had put his sword away, but Penelope didn't dare charge him. He looped his arms through the bag's drawstrings and hung it on his back.

"You will be carrying that bag," he said, pointing. "I won't risk you running off with your friends."

Penelope looked at where he pointed. A pack sat on the floor where he had been. It was oddly heavy as she picked it up, frowning. How was she going to carry it with only one hand?

"Where did you get this, anyway?" she asked, setting it back down. Maybe she could loop her belt through it.

Finnegan smiled smugly. "I've been here long enough to have my own caches of supplies. Raven's not the only one."

Penelope struggled to undo her belt one-handedly, loop it through the straps of the pack, and then redo it, but she managed. She used her free arm to adjust its position to hang more to the side. Even though this made her feel lopsided, it was better than constantly hitting the backs of her legs.

Finnegan watched her struggle with his arms folded across his chest. He didn't offer help, but Penelope wouldn't have let him even if he tried. Once she was done, he gestured out of the cave.

"We should bring the blanket with us," Penelope said, nodding toward the barrier they'd put up.

"No."

Well, there wasn't much point arguing with that. Penelope shook her head and headed out of the cave. The sun was bright again, but her feet sank deep into the soggy ground.

She couldn't see either the top of the mountain or down it. They were in such a heavily forested area. How close to the new springs were they? Were their classmates any closer to finding them? By now, she was confident they would have sent a message to the Institute to call for backup.

How much time did she have before getting to the new springs? How much time would it take for the Institute to find them?

"Now that we're here," Finnegan drawled, "let's see that dragon form of yours."

Penelope groaned. "How many times do I have to tell you I can't? Look at this shoulder. Whether it's physical or mental, the result is the same. I can't do it. If I could, I would have taken my dragon form last night and thrown you out of the cave rather than letting you take my friends prisoner."

This, finally, seemed to get through to Finnegan. His brows creased, and he looked at her shoulder again. He seemed to hesitate, then shrugged. "There are plants up near the spring that will help with your pain."

"Thanks," Penelope muttered sarcastically. Her braid hung limply down her back as she picked her way out of the mud. "Why didn't you drink from the Silver Springs that summer when you took us all prisoner?"

Finnegan followed her. She expected him to tell her to move faster, but he didn't. "You wouldn't understand."

"Probably not," Penelope agreed. "But I'm just curious whether you ever asked to be allowed to drink."

"Why should I ask when I knew the answer was no? Eldavon doesn't let anyone drink from the springs other than their own people," Finnegan replied.

Usually, he would sound bitter. Today, though, he just seemed... tired.

Penelope hesitated as she found firm ground. A massive flood of rain appeared to have come down practically in a line. While the mud below was slick and slippery, the ground was moist but not so deep that it sucked her feet in.

She tapped her feet against a tree to knock the mud off her shoes.

"I can't say I know much about the politics of it all," she said slowly, "but I'm pretty sure Odeutla has harder stratifications than Eldavon."

Finnegan drew his sword to flick the mud off his own shoes. "And just what is that supposed to mean?"

"I mean, let's look at us here," she said, pointing first to herself and then the bookbag. "Kaia's parents are all in the government. Nolen and I both come from families that work on various Watches. Wickham's mother is a seamstress, and his father is a carpenter. Herja is an orphan."

"So?"

"So, none of that prevented us from being brought into the Institute," Penelope replied. "We all had the same basic education. Schooling, healthcare, shelter, and food; it's all supplied by the Crown. A child can be born into any circumstances and get to any position they want to be. But in Odentia, you have generational poverty."

Finnegan pointed the sword toward a narrow deer trail. "Let's get going. I don't want to hear about your bleeding heart."

Penelope started walking, going slower than she strictly needed to. Partly to delay them and partly because if Finnegan wanted her to go faster, she wanted to have room to pacify him.

"If you do end up with powers like Raven's, what will you do to us?" she asked as she picked her way over the trail. "Are you going to kill us all?"

"Once I have what I want, you'll be free to go as long as you don't try to stop me."

Penelope glanced over her shoulder, frowning. He seemed to be genuine... but could she really trust it?

He was panting, skin taking on a sheen of sweat. He was using his sword as a walking stick and was so engrossed in what he was doing that she could easily disarm him...

But what then? He still had the bookbag and all her friends inside. So instead of attacking, Penelope stepped off the trail and found a good-sized stick that she picked up.

"Here," she said, holding it out as Finnegan passed her.

His head snapped up. The sword flicked up toward her neck, but Penelope refused to flinch.

"You can use this as a walking stick," she said, stepping back onto the trail.

Finnegan bared his teeth. It reminded her suddenly of a coyote she'd once rescued from a fire barricade. It had gotten stuck in the bramble and growled and snapped at her as she tried to free it. But it had only been afraid...

Was Finnegan afraid?

"You know we don't want to hurt you, right?" she said as he took the walking stick.

"Shut up."

Penelope tilted her head to the side, trying to figure him out. He had to realize that if they really wanted to hurt him, they would have done so already.

"You're sick," she said, approaching it from a different angle. "If we went back to camp—"

"I'm not going back. My brother wants magic for our kingdom. We will have magic," Finnegan muttered.

What was driving him so hard? Penelope churned over the possibilities. Maybe the answer to all their problems was finding a solution to Finnegan of Odentia's problem.

⬥

HERJA WAS LYING on the barrels. She knew it wasn't really fair that the others had been giving her more room than they'd been taking themselves. Kaia, Raven, and Wickham were all sitting while Nolen was stretched out over their feet. It had to be even more uncomfortable than laying atop these barrels...

But she couldn't find it in herself to tell them she could switch.

Her eyes were closed, one hand over them to help block out the light from the light stones integrated into the walls.

"It feels like we're vertical," Kaia said after some time. The entire bag had been swaying slightly for some hours.

Even though Herja had had various witches put spells on it so that the interior was stable despite what the exterior was doing, there were still subtle pressures that they had to contend with.

"We should start planning how to get out again," Wickham said. "We don't know when Finnegan will lose his temper with Penelope."

"We have heard no shouting, though," Kaia said.

Nolen made a soft sort of noise. "Doesn't mean he won't lose his temper with her."

"I agree with Kaia," Raven whispered. "I know he was putting on a show for me, but he always would have verbal outbursts before doing anything else."

Herja rolled over with difficulty. She swallowed hard as she gazed at where Raven's hidden face was. She wished they knew if Raven's eyes or her whole face held the magic to turn things to stone. "Did he hurt you?"

Raven shook their head. "He yelled sometimes, but he never hurt me."

Herja opened her mouth when suddenly they all lurched to the side. It sent her flying off the barrels, and she landed hard on the others' knees. The air was driven from her lungs, and pain shot through her.

She pushed herself up, trying to avoid hurting the others. "What happened?"

Raven moved to the entrance and tugged on the opening, widening it. "Wickham, you're needed."

"What?" Herja demanded.

Sounds of coughing came from outside. Wickham crawled toward the entrance.

"Wait," Herja called, but Wickham didn't listen.

Praying nothing went wrong, Herja followed—she would not let her fated mate face Finnegan alone!

# CHAPTER
# TWENTY-THREE

WICKHAM WRIGGLED out of the narrow opening of the book bag, looking up cautiously. He half expected that he'd find a sword in his face, but instead, he looked at a completely different scene.

Finnegan was half-slumped on a rocky outcropping, his sword in hand. It appeared he was trying to point it at Penelope, but the tip was pointed more toward the ground. Penelope sat on the ground some distance away, her eyes shut as her face rapidly shifted from white to green.

"What happened?" Wickham demanded, hurrying toward his friend.

"Get back in—" Finnegan hunched over as explosive coughs shook his body.

Wickham ignored him for the time being, focused on Penelope. She had cracked one eye open to look at him but closed it again.

"I slipped," she moaned.

Wickham caught her as she slumped toward the ground. From the leaves on her broken shoulder, it was clear what happened. He winced as he helped her down, clearing the ground beneath her. Better for her to be lying down than risk falling.

"I don't have anything for the pain," he said, grimacing. All he could do was put his hands over her shoulder and pray out a spell.

Her skin was hot and inflamed. Not good. He let his hands hover over her skin, not touching. He could still feel the heat radiating off her. Closing his eyes, he prayed with all his might that she would have relief.

When he opened his eyes, her eyes were still shut, but her breathing was a little easier. As a healer, all he could work with was his own energy and Penelope's... and clearly, giving her even this much relief had wiped her out.

"Give that back, girl," Finnegan wheezed behind them.

Wickham took off his jacket and laid it over Penelope to keep her warm before he turned. Finnegan was still on the outcropping, but his sword had been replaced by a knife.

Herja stood a short distance away, the sword in her hand now.

"You don't even know how to use that," Finnegan said.

Wickham hurried over to Herja. "I need to check him—he's not in good shape."

Herja held the sword by the hilt, twisting the point into the ground. "As long as he promises not to attack you," she said, but a pucker was in her eyebrows. "Put the knife away. You're clearly not in shape to fight; believe it or not, we are trying to help."

"Get back in the bag!" Finnegan snapped.

Wickham stepped forward, holding both hands to indicate he was unarmed. "You can hardly breathe—I have something that will help with the coughing. It's actually a bit of a specialty of mine. A couple of years ago, my father was sick with water in his lungs, and I learned how to treat it."

Finnegan opened his mouth, presumably to snap at him, but only groaned. He lowered the knife and gestured Wickham forward with this other hand.

"Herja, can you check on Penelope, please?" Wickham said as he moved forward, slowly but confidently.

"She goes back into the bag," Finnegan snapped.

Wickham shook his head as he reached into the bag at his waist.

He drew out a mint camphor and offered it to their captor. Although he wasn't much of a captor right now.

"I need help, and Herja is my fated mate," Wickham replied.

Finnegan grumbled again but nodded.

As Wickham continued to look through his bag for what else might help, Finnegan took the camphor and sucked on it. His dark eyes never left Wickham, squinting suspiciously.

The funny thing was that Finnegan had to be six or seven years older than Wickham, yet despite the situation, Wickham wasn't afraid of him. Maybe it was foolish or just the 'doctor brain,' as Kassandra put it. He had a patient to tend to, and he would tend to them.

"I'm going to help Pen get into the bookbag so she can get some rest," Herja called to them.

Wickham nodded. "Good idea. It's no good for her shoulder to be moving around like that. See if Kaia and Nolen will come out to help look for herbs, will you?"

"I never said you could do that," Finnegan said.

Wickham drew some willow bark tea from his bag. It would help with Finnegan's fever. "Let's be honest, you aren't exactly in charge here, Finnegan. But I'm sure we can negotiate the situation."

Maybe they had a chance to resolve this—

But apparently, those words were a mistake, as Finnegan's hand rose. Before Wickham realized what was happening, the sharp edge of Finnegan's knife pressed against his neck. Wickham froze, his eyes widening.

Herja made a choked-off noise.

"I am in charge, boy," Finnegan hissed. "And you had better not forget it."

Wickham's hands shook, but he still managed to say, "I'm sorry."

"You can take the girl into the bag," Finnegan said toward Herja. "But nobody else comes out."

"Understood," Herja said, sounding subdued.

Finnegan lowered the knife again.

Wickham took a moment to orient himself again, reminding himself what he was doing. He inhaled deeply as he started to mix some herbs. "I need a fire to make the tea, and I really will need help collecting more herbs."

"Then you can take your scowling friend with you. But no others." Finnegan waved the knife in his face again. "I'll start the fire and water boiling while you're gone. But if I get so much as a hint that you have betrayed me, I'll throw your friends into the river."

And this time, Wickham had to believe him. He couldn't even convince Finnegan there was a better way about it, either—Finnegan didn't want to negotiate.

That much was clear.

⁂

DESPITE SEEING FINNEGAN THREATEN WICKHAM, Herja found she managed to keep calm. At least she wasn't doing anything foolish like trying to attack Finnegan.

It helped, she mused, that Finnegan wasn't anywhere in sight anymore.

She and Wickham had been searching the forest for the herbs he needed for fifteen minutes so far. Herja had remained quiet so far if only because she was afraid Finnegan would hear them and be offended by what she wanted to say.

Eventually, Wickham sighed. "Looks like there's some frost lichen here. That'll be useful to have."

Herja stepped around him to peer at the lichen. Then, she let out a breath. "Try not to provoke him."

"I didn't try to provoke him at all," Wickham said.

"I didn't say you were trying to provoke him; I said try not to provoke him."

Wickham shook his head. "I guess I just have to keep my guard up. He might be sick, but he will not trust us just because we want to help.'"

Herja carefully scraped the frost lichen into her palm, as Wickham had taught her. "He has no proof that we actually want to help. And to him, we don't. We want to stop him from reaching the springs. That's all he cares about."

"I don't like his brother." Wickham searched through some grasses, then added, "Now that I've gotten a closer look at him, I think this might be a chronic illness. Not from the storms, although I can't imagine that helped. And he's smaller than he should be... chronic malnutrition, maybe. Although maybe I'm reading too much into it."

"From what I know about him and Odentia? It wouldn't surprise me." Herja stepped around the tree and spotted a raspberry bush. She hurried to it, her stomach rumbling.

There were only a handful of berries, and she put one in her mouth, then returned to Wickham. Once he saw her chewing, he took all of them, just as she intended. He popped the berries into his mouth and closed his eyes.

"It's still not an excuse for his behavior," Herja said, keeping the mushed raspberry on her tongue.

"No, but maybe it's something that we can work with to get him to realize what he's doing is wrong," Wickham said.

Herja frowned doubtfully. "Or anything we say about it, he'll take as a personal attack and kill us."

"Obviously, we don't just demand outright if he's been mistreated," Wickham said.

"How is that obvious?" Herja kicked the ground.

Wickham turned to her, a furrow in his brow. He reached out toward her, then hesitated. "Can I give you a hug?"

"I... don't know. I want you to, but I also don't want to be touched right now," Herja admitted.

Wickham, bless him, nodded seriously. He folded his arms around himself and hugged tightly. "Air hugs, then."

Herja mimicked him. Weirdly, it did help her to feel better. Some of the stiffness eased out of her body.

"I know it's hard," Wickham murmured softly. "We're all afraid... but it's okay for you to say what you're feeling, even if you know we all feel the same way."

Herja hugged herself tighter. "Thank you. Now we should get back."

Wickham nodded, his eyes never leaving her. A strange warmth filled her chest, and she dropped her arms. No, not when her friends were in danger.

She turned away quickly. The two were quiet as they trekked back to where Finnegan waited. When they arrived, He was asleep on the edge of the book bag. Wickham sighed as he started forward, but Herja caught his arm.

Moving as quietly as she could, she crept forward, heart in her throat. If she could get the bookbag away from him—

But Finnegan, without opening his eyes, moved it to his other side. "Don't even think about it."

Herja fell back. He hadn't retrieved the sword, and she went to it as Wick started to mix the herbs into his tea.

"Where did you get this?" Herja asked as she frowned at it.

Before, she thought she had felt something... off about the sword. Now she was sure of it.

Finnegan opened his eyes. "What?"

"The sword." She turned it to inspect the blade. Rust was showing in some spots... As she leaned in closer, she smelled the distinctive iron scent. "It's not steel. It's iron... Odentia uses steel to forge their weapons."

Finnegan pushed himself to a sitting position, frowning at her. "What are you talking about?"

"Odentia has incredible metalworking magic," she said with a shrug. "Why are you using this piece of junk?"

"Odentia doesn't have magic. We use our brains for metalworking... something that you Eldavon idiot don't know how to do, apparently." Finnegan got shakily to his feet and stalked over to her.

He had the book bag and a knife, so she handed the sword over without a word. He was right; they weren't equipped to take him on when he had any sort of strength to him... part of her wished they could have drugged him with the herbs they found.

She also knew Wickham would never think about drugging a patient unless it was best for them, and they consented.

"Next time, go for the blow instead of asking stupid questions," Finnegan said as he glared down at her.

"It's only stupid if the answer isn't important. But it is important. Not only is it iron, but it's got magic attached to it." Herja rubbed the back of her neck as she frowned at the sword. "Did you dunk it in the springs? Or is there something else... does it talk to you?"

Finnegan's jaw dropped. "What are you going on about?"

Herja's cheeks warmed, but she tried not to show her embarrassment. "I just read a story about an evil sword that possesses the people who use it. But I don't think that sort of magic actually exists. Most likely, it's picked up something from the mountain."

"You have three choices," Finnegan growled as he raised the sword and rested it against her shoulder. "Shut up, get into the bag, or die. Which will you pick?"

Herja pressed her lips together. Her heart hammered harder as she desperately wished she had the skills to disarm this man. But even when she held a sword, and he only had a knife, she felt any attacks wouldn't go well for her.

Finnegan grabbed her shoulder, shoved her toward Wickham, and then returned to his previous spot.

*I wish Row were here.* They'd know what to do. About Finnegan. About Raven. They'd fix this. But they weren't here... so what was she going to do?

# CHAPTER
# TWENTY-FOUR

WICKHAM GLANCED over the trail to where Herja struggled through the thick brush. While Finnegan was allowing Wickham to walk right in front of him—with the provision of having his hands loosely tied in front of him, Herja had to stay off the path but in Finnegan's sight.

"Maybe we should take a break," Wickham suggested, not just because Herja was struggling.

Behind him, Finnegan was also starting to pant audibly, despite the slower pace Wickham was walking at. Over the last few hours, he realized that the more tired Finnegan got, the more unpredictable he was.

"And why do you think we should have a break?" Finnegan wheezed.

Wickham resisted the urge to roll his eyes. It should be obvious, but Finnegan didn't like it when they suggested he might be sick or weak. Of course, Wickham didn't dare say this aloud... though Finnegan seemed more agreeable here than he had in the Silent Marshes, he was still unpredictable.

"Let me rephrase that," Wickham said, half-turning to their captor. "May we take a break? I'm not used to climbing these steep trails, and my legs are tired."

"Fine," Finnegan grumbled, then sank onto a nearby fallen log.

Herja approached. She carried both the supply pack and the book-bag. Sweat dripped from her nose as she gestured to the waterskin on Wickham's belt. "Can I?"

"Go ahead," Finnegan allowed.

Wickham handed Herja the waterskin. "We're making good time. I think we've gone farther this last hour than we did all day yesterday."

Herja drank the water deeply, then wiped her mouth with her hand. "I have a few theories about that. I think either the spring is letting us come to it because Prince Finnegan is sick, or it has something to do with the sword."

It had been an unspoken agreement that they both referred to Finnegan as 'prince' when they spoke about him aloud. Referring to him by his title seemed to mollify him.

Wickham turned to frown at the sword hanging from Finnegan's belt. "The sword?"

"It's magic," Herja said. "I don't know how, but it is."

Finnegan was sucking on another camphor now. He cocked his head to the side and smiled. "I took it from the Eldavon prison when I escaped. Your so-called guards are weak. If it had been an Odentian prison, I never would have been able to get out."

"Yeah, because they'd have been starving you to death," Herja replied snarkily.

Wickham groaned. "Herja."

She folded her arms. "What? It's true. I don't understand why he's so eager to impress his brother when his brother threw him in prison in the first place. I mean, why not put him in some remote palace and call him exiled?"

"Don't talk about my brother; you can't possibly understand."

"But what are you really after?" Herja pressed. "Can you honestly say your brother will welcome you back if you have magic? He doesn't seem to care about you—"

"I said don't talk about him!" Finnegan struggled back to his feet and pointed down the path. "Break's over. Back at it."

Herja and Wickham exchanged glances, then Herja moved back off the path. Wickham started walking, shaking his head. They'd be at the springs soon, and what were they supposed to do then?

⁂

PENELOPE WASN'T REALLY ASLEEP, not between the light and pain. Through the help of the others, she could find a position that at least didn't make it worse, but this was only getting worse...

Kaia, Nolen, and Raven were playing a card game just to occupy their hands when Raven let out a low gasp. In just that single noise, Penelope heard genuine fear. Her eyes snapped open—they were here. She didn't have to ask. The gentle swaying of the bag had stopped.

Nolen hurried to the entrance and glanced at Penelope. "How's the shoulder?"

"Hurts," Penelope whispered back. She grimaced as she tried to move it. She couldn't.

"But you shouldn't," Wickham's voice came from outside, sounding stressed.

"I said shut up," Finnegan yelled back.

Penelope's heart slammed into her throat. They had to do something! Everything they'd talked about being able to do rested on delaying this moment... but they were here now and couldn't just sit back and leave Herja and Wickham out there!

The bookbag lurched, showing they had been put down.

Good. That gave them a chance to escape. Herja and Wickham were arguing with Finnegan. From his tone of voice, he was getting angrier... not good. But perhaps. Something they could use to their advantage?

"We have to get out there," Penelope whispered.

"And do what?" Raven asked, sounding stressed. "Threaten him with me? He won't believe it."

"For all we know, Raven being sick is why they were touched so strongly by the magic," Wickham said outside. "There's a reason the children have to climb Mount Eldavon before they can drink from the Silver Springs. Because if you're too weak, the magic will damage you."

A lie. Penelope struggled to get into a sitting position. The weakness in her shoulder and arm was getting even worse, working down her body.

Finnegan made a furious noise. "I'm not an idiot! Get out of the way!"

Kaia pushed her way between Penelope and Nolen. She pushed a finger out of the tightly bound entrance of the bookbag and tugged on the strings, bringing them inside. "Does anyone have a knife?"

"No," Penelope groaned.

Nolen shook his head, and Raven was silent.

Kaia struggled with the string. As she did so, Penelope closed her eyes. She reached inside, looking for that flame that had come so easily the first time she shifted to her dragon form. What had pulled it out of reach? Other dragons had suffered worse injuries than this and could still shift—was something wrong with her?

"Clearly, you can get past us if you try," Wickham said stubbornly. Penelope could almost see his chin raised. "You're armed. We're not. So please, just listen. Penelope rescued you from the kelpie in the Silent Marshes. I've freely offered to help with your injuries. We are not your enemies here!"

"But I am your enemy," Finnegan hissed back.

Herja spoke. "Maybe you don't have to be."

"Shut up! The girl here said the spring will heal me, so enough nonsense about me being too weak."

"But are you prepared to take the cost of it?" Herja asked, her voice very soft.

Kaia let out a small cry of triumph.

Penelope's eyes snapped back open. The witch had managed to untangle the knot of strings and was currently opening the entrance up wide.

"Finnegan made a mistake," Kaia whispered as she drew her wand from her belt. "He gave us time to rest and recover our strength."

She pointed the wand at Penelope's shoulder. Penelope opened her mouth to stop her—she couldn't fight Finnegan, but with Kaia's magic, she might be able to do something. She couldn't waste her strength—but Kaia was already speaking.

"Let this cloth become as stone, protecting Penelope's shoulder while weighing nothing more," she intoned.

Nothing seemed to change. But the cloth around her shoulder felt... stronger. When she reached up to touch it, the bandages felt like a plaster cast, keeping her shoulder in place.

"Should have thought of that earlier," Kaia mumbled, "let's stop him. Once and for all."

Nolen slipped out of the bag. As Kaia moved to follow, Penelope stopped her. "Finnegan hates you most of all—stay here and be safe."

Penelope used her one arm to claw her way out of the book bag. She stumbled to her feet, adrenaline pulsing as she took in the sight.

A small puddle of water sat bubbling in the cleft of a rock. The water disappeared back into the stone while two enormous cliffs sat riding up on either side. The sky was utterly black, flickering with blue and yellow lightning, and yet no sound of thunder.

Herja and Wickham stood near the spring, their backs to it as Finnegan faced them, the sword clutched in both hands. Nolen leaped at him, but Finnegan must have heard him coming. He turned, dodged Nolen's reach, and slashed at the dragon across the chest.

Nolen fell back as the screech of iron meeting iron filled the air. Nolen's shirt was torn, revealing steel-grey scales beneath.

"So that's how it is, is it?" Finnegan roared as he lifted the sword above his head, turning to Penelope. "Fine—if I have to kill all of you, so be it!"

Penelope lifted her hand. "But you don't."

Finnegan panted, staring at her as though her words froze him.

"You don't," Penelope repeated. "Think about it. We're teenagers who haven't even tried to hurt you. Can you honestly say violence is necessary?"

"You're just trying to confuse me." Finnegan's expression hardened. "I'm too close to give up now!"

STAY INSIDE, and don't get into trouble.

Kaia knew that was wise. But some compulsion brought her out when she heard Nolen's grunt of pain. She crawled from the bookbag, glanced around once, and rushed to her mate's side. His shirt was cleanly cut, a pale scale-like pattern disappearing from his skin.

"Kaia!" Penelope yelled. "I told you—"

Finnegan roared as he leaped forward, swinging the sword. Kaia snatched up a stick nearby as the fallen prince aimed a blow at Penelope. Kaia jammed it beneath his knees, tripping him. He went sprawling; the sword flying from his hand.

A whisper ran across the back of her neck. The sense of something deep, some connection flowed from the ground into her. She was distracted from Finnegan, her eyes moving to the springs.

It was as though each bubble was a tired exhale. Like there was something here, something that wanted to speak to her. But what was it saying?

"Kaia!" Nolen shouted.

Something cold pressed against her neck. Pain shot through her, and she stiffened, her jaw dropping in a silent scream. For a second, she was sure that Finnegan had cut her neck, that she'd feel her blood gushing out any moment.

"I need that spring," Finnegan said. His voice was filled with fury and fear, and desperation.

Nolen scrambled to his feet. At some point, Raven had left the bookbag; they stood with Penelope, Herja, and Wickham, blocking the path to the spring.

Finnegan dragged Kaia to her feet, keeping the knife on her. "You'll let me pass now, or I'll kill her. And you know I will."

Magic coursed in the air. Not good, not bad. Just... there. Kaia shuffled forward with Finnegan as the others reluctantly stepped out of the way. The bubbling grew more intense. Words started to form in Kaia's mind.

. . .

*HERE AGELESS SOULS DO MOAN, here restless dead do roam.*
  *Bring down the mountain's weight. Let them find their peace.*
  *Give the dead their sleep at last within the darkness deep.*
  *Lay their heads upon the grave and cover them with stone.*

HER HEART POUNDED as Finnegan drew closer, bringing her with him. The bubbling sounded like cries for help now.

"Do you hear them?" she whispered.

"Hear what?" Finnegan snapped.

Raven spoke. "I do. I can hear them."

"Oh, it's another trick, is it?" Finnegan snarled. He tightened his hold on Kaia as he dragged the stone toward the spring. It was as though steps were carved into it.

The others were talking, but Kaia didn't hear them. Her eyes were transfixed on the water. It was pale, silvery-blue, and as she looked deeper, there seemed to be a face inside of it. Goosebumps formed over her arms.

Ageless souls. Bring down the mountain's weight... Her eyes were transfixed on the rocky outcropping above the springs. Could she...?

# CHAPTER
# TWENTY-FIVE

HERJA HELD HER BREATH, her heart pounding in her chest. She couldn't take her eyes off the knife pressed against Kaia's throat. She kept expecting blood at any moment. Every hitch of Finnegan's breath made her wince.

It wasn't even that Finnegan's unpredictable nature and hair trigger made his animosity with Kaia especially dangerous. But Finnegan was weak. He could stumble or falter and accidentally cut Kaia's throat open.

They were only a few feet from the new springs now. They had no choice but to allow him to drink, didn't they?

She held the sword in her hands, having retrieved it after Finnegan dropped it. The metal warmed beneath her skin.

Any wrong move would end Kaia's life. Herja opened her mouth but shut it again. Threatening Finnegan would do no good.

"Please, let her go," Nolen urged. His voice was raspy as he shifted from foot to foot. "Please."

"No. You're going to try to stop me. I can't allow this."

"But—" Penelope said, her tone pleading.

Herja held an arm out in front of her other friends. "I don't think we want to distract him. Look at the way he's shaking."

Finnegan narrowed his eyes at her, briefly stopping his approach. "What's that supposed to mean?"

"Nothing. Only that you could hurt Kaia accidentally." Herja swallowed hard as she finally tore her eyes from the knife. "What will you do to us once you have magic?"

Finnegan grinned. "That depends on the magic, doesn't it?"

Kaia made a mewling noise.

"But if you're planning on killing us anyway, killing Kaia, then is there a point in us trying to save her?" Herja continued. She made her voice as flat as possible.

Nolen growled at her as Wickham gave her a horrified look, but Herja glanced at Penelope with a significant glance, and the other dragon understood.

"She has a good point. If you plan to kill us all anyway, why shouldn't we all just die to stop you?" Penelope asked.

"If I wanted to kill you, I'd have done it already," Finnegan hissed. "Do you really think that I'm stupid? I could have had you all go into that bag and pinned you underwater. I could have drowned you all easily. I've been trying to give you stupid children the chance to escape this without being harmed."

"Why should we believe that when you tried to kill Kaia in the swamp?" Wickham demanded.

Finnegan glared at the witch, starting his journey backward again. "So much for Eldavon's assurances of accepting a change of heart. It's unfair that a bunch of useless children like you have magic, and I am denied it."

Herja stepped forward, the sword still in her hands. "And there's nothing more of this debate we can say. We stand on opposite sides... but maybe we can help you drink from the Silver Springs."

The others shifted uncomfortably.

"What?" Herja turned to them. "It's better than this spring, isn't it? We don't know what sort of magic this is. We'd all be better off if Finnegan drank from the Silver Springs."

THEY WEREN'T GOING to change Finnegan's mind. Wickham knew that. He knew Finnegan would drink, but what would happen next? The magic here felt off. It wasn't... *right*. It didn't feel evil, just... somehow, it seemed sad.

How could magic be sad?

His eyes locked on Kaia. The other witch wasn't paying attention to the conversation. Her eyes were locked on the springs, a pucker in her brow like she was figuring something out.

They couldn't change Finnegan's mind—but maybe there was a chance for Kaia to reach whatever conclusion she was struggling for.

"What if you already have magic?" Wickham blurted.

Finnegan inched back, all the while glaring at him.

"Humans have magic," Wickham insisted. "Maybe not as flashy as witches and dragons, but their magic is just as important. Without humans, we'd fall apart."

Finnegan replied with a derisive snort.

"If you really don't want to hurt us, there's no reason to," Wickham said, holding out his hands. "Come back to camp with us. We will get you healed again. You're sick, but even in our prisons, you'll receive the care you need."

"I know what sort of prisons you have, boy. And I don't care what you say. Would you have been so happy to be human instead of a witch?"

Wickham sighed. "Honestly? I wanted to be human. When I drank, and my hair turned silver, I was miserable. I didn't recognize myself in the mirror. Only after I realized I could be a healer, I started to accept it... and sometimes it's still difficult."

Finnegan took a deep breath. "But you had the choice. Why is it so wrong that I want that choice, too? And if humans are so revered in your culture, why do witches and dragons have a special school catered to their needs?"

166

"Because it is a need," Herja replied at once. Nolen, Raven, and Penelope were quiet like they recognized that, despite the situation, Herja and Wickham were the ones who would most likely reach Finnegan.

Most likely. And they had very little chance at that.

"Humans also have schools. Multiple schools," Herja said. "We all have different needs. Or would you say that the humans studying at the medical academies are treated as superior because they have a specialized medical school?"

Finnegan was silent.

Wickham took a deep breath, edging forward. "Half of our kings and queens are human."

"And yet your human king and queen are replaced more often," Finnegan growled.

"Not true," Herja said.

Finnegan shook his head. "It doesn't matter. Do you really think you can change my mind? Give me the sword back. Then I'll let you all leave. But I'm keeping Miss Mouthy here to make sure that you and your teachers don't stop me."

Wickham turned to Herja. Her eyes met his, and he saw the question: what should she do?

A BITTER TASTE filled Kaia's mouth as Herja's shoulders slumped. Her silver eyes slid from Wickham to Kaia, and the uncertainty in her eyes disappeared.

"You want it? Fine. Just don't hurt her."

"Herja," Kaia started, but Finnegan shook her, making her fall silent.

Herja tossed the sword, hilt-first, toward Finnegan. The knife at her throat left as Finnegan reached forward to grab it. His fingers slipped over the hilt, and the sword tumbled past him, landing squarely in the springs.

A noise somewhere between a hiss and a sigh filled the air. Finnegan lurched, showing he heard it, too.

Kaia seized his momentary distraction. Her trembling hand reached into the pouch at her waist, and she withdrew the wand Nolen had made her so long ago. Her fingers clasped the polished handle as she withdrew it, hiding it in the folds of her skirt as she did so.

Finnegan's cursing momentarily made her heart seize. The knife returned to her throat. He'd noticed. The game was up. He'd kill her and—

"Fine, I'll just get it when I drink," he yelled.

Kaia turned her head slightly. Finnegan glared at Herja as though she'd intentionally thrown the sword into the springs.

Now was her chance.

Kaia took a deep breath, hoping this wouldn't end with any of them dead, and turned her wand over in her hand so that it was discreetly pointing upward toward a rocky outcropping.

"*Here ageless souls do moan, here restless dead do roam,*" she chanted under her breath.

"What are you saying?" Finnegan demanded, dragging her back another few feet.

"*Bring down the mountain's weight. Let them find their peace. Give the dead their sleep at last within the darkness deep.*" Kaia lifted her arm, pointing her wand at the rocky outcroppings. "*Lay their heads upon the grave and cover them with stone.*"

A crack filled the air, thundering like the storms. Lightning flared in the sky, bolts of it arching from the black clouds. They stuck the outcropping. More thunderous noises, and then, the rock moved. It slid away from the side of the mountain, cleanly severed.

Kaia's heart jumped to her throat. It worked!

Then the first stones rumbled toward them, and her heart froze.

The landslide was going to bury them all.

She'd condemned her friends to death.

⚜

FINNEGAN LET OUT A ROUGH CRY, shoving Kaia away as he leaped for the springs. The rocks ground against the other side of the cleft, grinding to a halt. Penelope could see from where she was that they were caught on a small nub on the other side—it wouldn't last long.

"We have to get out of here," she shouted, darting forward.

Kaia wrapped her arms around Finnegan's chest, trying to pull him back.

"Let me go," he howled, knife forgotten. He clawed at Kaia's hands, trying to make her release him.

It was a sign of just how bad of shape he was in, if Kaia could drag him back.

"No!" Finnegan screamed again. "No, I can't go back without magic! I need it! *Please!*"

Wickham joined Kaia, helping her to pull Finnegan back.

Penelope snatched up the book bag and whirled to Nolen and Herja, who seemed frozen.

"Shift," Penelope yelled at them. "We need to get out of here!"

She reached deep inside of her. A flicker of flame seemed to erupt in the center of her chest, and with a cry of relief, she shifted to her turquoise dragon form. The cloth bandages twisted and expanded with her, working off Kaia's spell. They kept her arm locked against her chest.

A flash of light erupted from Nolen. In the blink of an eye, he stood towering over them in a steel-grey form, his scales interlocking in plated armor. A heavy club sat at the end of his tail. He grabbed Kaia and Finnegan in his hands as Raven climbed onto Penelope's back. A sharp cracking noise came from the cliffs. The rocks plummeted once more.

Penelope was frozen for half a second. The sight was magnificent, those massive blocks of rock hurtling through the air. Terrifying, deadly... but magnificent.

"Move!" Wickham shouted.

Penelope wheeled about and leaped into the air. The rocks came crashing down behind them, the shockwaves knocking into Penelope.

She struggled in the sudden gusts of wind to stay upright as she beat her wings, angling herself down the mountain.

Nolen's massive grey form spread his wings to one side of her, Kaia and Finnegan both clutched in his hands.

On her other side, Wickham rode on Herja's back. As the rocks groaned and thundered behind them, Penelope took a moment to admire her friend's sleek form.

Herja's dragon was clad in scales so small it looked like she had smooth skin. Starting at royal blue along her belly, her coloring morphed to a rich amethyst along her sides and finally to an emerald green along her back. The breathtaking gradient gave her the image of rippling waves. Unlike Penelope and Nolen, she had no weaponry on her.

Penelope could have laughed—until a strange tugging started in her chest. The flames she'd finally reached withdrew. Her wings shrank against her, and she struggled to maintain forward momentum.

She plummeted, Raven's scream echoing behind her. Nolen and Herja dodged in together, trying to help the two falling students.

They crashed into each other, jostling Wickham off Herja's shoulders.

A fresh gust of wind brought torrential rainfall on them as Herja flipped over, grabbing Wickham and Raven with her foot. Penelope's wings were still big enough to angle herself downward as the wind and rain blinded her.

And somewhere from the tallest peaks of the mountain, the rocs howled in fury.

# CHAPTER
# TWENTY-SIX

THE GUSTS of wind drove their little group to the ground. Wickham's fingers scraped over Herja's tiny scales, trying to find a purchase that wasn't there. He pitched suddenly to the side and, with a gush of wind, slid down her back, landing in a tangled heap of limbs.

He kept his head bowed as he struggled to his feet. He didn't dare look up, for fear the rocs would catch him in their mesmer once more. The rain buffeted him as he struggled to make out the shapes of his friend in the downpour.

His drenched clothes clung to his body as the wind chilled him to the bone. He fought to regain his footing amid the relentless gusts of wind. A flash of red caught his eye—Penelope. Wickham stumbled toward her as she collapsed, a dark figure lurking over her. Raven or Finnegan?

Wickham slid on a patch of mud, sliding down the mountainside to knock into the figure. It was Raven, but the impact sent them rolling away.

Finnegan stood nearby, and his face turned upward. He was transfixed by the majestic and deadly rocs soaring overhead.

"Wick," Penelope gasped.

She pressed Herja's bookbag into his hand, then collapsed against it. He couldn't see her clearly through the rain, but Wickham knew she must be in terrible pain. The wet bag in his hands weighed heavily; with that, he knew what to do.

With no sign of the others, he slipped and slid toward Finnegan. Lifting the bag in his hands, he made one last jump, bringing the bookbag down over Finnegan's head.

The Odentian prince jerked and shouted, but Wickham was too fast. He yanked the bookbag down, swallowing Finnegan whole. Then he knotted the strings and threw it over his back, hoping the rain wouldn't leak inside.

A hand grabbed his arm, making him cry out. But when he turned, it was Herja. She gripped his arm as the rocs screamed above them. The thunderous beats of their wings drew closer. Herja dragged Wickham back to the others, all gathered around Penelope.

"Drop," Herja yelled, her voice raising above the sound of the storm. "Raven, look up—uncover your face!"

Wickham threw himself to the muddy ground instantly. He covered his head with his hands, praying with all his might that this would work.

For a moment, there was only silence. It was as though the storm itself had frozen and turned to stone at seeing Raven's face.

Then there was a final cry from the rocs. A fresh gust of wind burst over them, but once it was over, the rain had lessened to a heavy deluge rather than flooding. Wickham didn't dare raise his head, not yet. Not until—

"It's over," Raven called. "You can look up again."

Wickham slowly lifted his head. His eyes immediately searched for his friends. Penelope still lay face-up, her expression twisted in pain. Nolen and Kaia were getting to their knees, covered in mud and holding one another. Herja was already on her feet, gesturing to Raven to help her get Penelope to her feet.

They were all right. Wickham took a deep breath as he shoved himself to his feet. He looked around warily, but no sign of the rocs— stone or living.

There wasn't time to dwell on that, in any case. Wickham hurried over to Herja and helped to stabilize Penelope. Her head fell forward as she groaned—the fall must have been even worse for her. Wickham flinched as he saw her shoulder jutting up at an odd angle.

"This way," Raven called.

They led the way, slipping occasionally, but their directions were confident. Nolen took over helping Herja with Penelope when Wickham nearly fell, so he and Kaia took up the end of their little group. The bookbag lay heavy on Wickham's back, and from time to time; he took it off and carried it upside down to ensure there wasn't too much water getting in there.

Although, he bet Finnegan would take it as their attempt to torture him.

The rain had reduced to little more than a drizzle by the time they reached a shelter. It wasn't much, just a slight rock overhang with a relatively level spot beneath it. They could expand the area that was safe from being rained on by putting up a few blankets.

Nolen lit a fire, but they would not dry off, and staying warm would be difficult.

"We can use the empty barrels for fuel," Kaia suggested while trying to figure out plans. "So that we at least have a nice hot fire without a lot of smoke."

"And what about Finnegan?" Herja asked.

Penelope was passed out along the edge of the overhang, her sleep clearly not restful. Her shoulder had to be killing her.

"We can tie him up?" Kaia suggested doubtfully.

Wickham listened to the bookbag. "I'm not sure that will be necessary—he's been coughing for a few minutes now... I'm sure he's going to be weak."

Nolen stirred their little fire. "I agree with Kaia. We let Finnegan out. We tear apart the barrels and burn them. But I want him bound for as long as he's out."

Herja nodded, looking at Wickham. "I don't think we should risk him attacking us. We've given him so many chances already, and he's only proven that he will take those chances and throw them back in our faces.

173

It was true. Wickham nodded, albeit somewhat reluctantly. He just had to remember that just because Finnegan was sick didn't mean he was helpless—or that he'd be grateful toward them.

"Raven?" Nolen asked, turning to them.

Raven was currently trying to squeeze the water from their face veil without revealing their face. "Hmm?"

"Are you all right with this plan?"

"I... well, I suppose so," Raven said, although they sounded doubtful.

Herja crouched near the bookbag, pulled the strings loose, and then opened it up. "Come out, Finnegan."

The top of the bag twitched a little, then Finnegan pulled himself out. He was drenched, the same as the rest of them, but his breath was more wheezing than breathing. Wickham might have thought he was faking, except his lips were blue-tinged, and his eyes were glassy.

Nolen quickly tied Finnegan's hands, and the Odentian warrior didn't fight him. Once that was done, Kaia and Raven emptied the bookbag of the barrels. The food was shared, and Nolen and Herja broke apart the barrels to add to the fire. Meanwhile, Wickham treated Finnegan's breathing the best he could.

"What are you even doing?" Finnegan grunted at him as Wickham tried to get him to drink a tea mixture for the new fever Finnegan had developed.

"Treating your illness, what else?" Wickham replied, annoyed.

Finnegan twisted his head when Wickham brought the tea to his mouth. "Leave me alone. It's bad enough that you stole my chance at magic. Why do you have to act as though I'm a helpless child? You're the children."

But his normal fury was missing. Instead, his voice was dull, like he had lost all the fight.

Wickham sighed. "When will you accept that we in Eldavon don't have the same attitude as you in Odentia?"

"It was my last chance," Finnegan said. "I'll never prove myself to my brother now."

"No, you won't," Raven agreed suddenly. "Because your brother is dead."

---

HERJA SLIPPED OFF THE BARREL—THEY were surprisingly difficult to break apart—and stared in shock at Raven. "What?"

Finnegan stared at Raven as well, his face blanched.

Raven's shoulders were hunched inward. "No, I didn't mean—"

"Why would you say that?" Wickham demanded. He sounded somewhere between confused and upset. "The last thing we need is for—"

"Shh." Herja went to Wickham, frowning at Raven and put a hand on his shoulder. "Something prompted you to stay that, Raven. So why?"

From what she remembered, Raven wasn't the type of person to say things like that just to hurt others. So unless they had changed significantly, or Finnegan had hurt them more than they let on... but Herja didn't believe it. There was just something about the way Raven had spoken...

"I don't know why," Raven muttered.

"How could you even know that?" Finnegan snapped, sounding more like himself—but there was still a tremble to his voice that hadn't been there before.

Raven put their hands beneath their veil, rubbing at their face. "The last time I slept, I dreamt about a crown sitting on a grave. Then it changed to a young woman chained to a throne amid storm clouds. The Odentia king's only child is a girl...."

Nolen made a disbelieving noise in his throat as he added pieces of the barrel to the fire. "Prophecy isn't possible. That sort of magic doesn't exist."

"Doesn't it?" Herja asked dryly. "What about the story of magic that turns a person to stone? Or drives off rocs? Raven has ancient magic... surely you felt it at the springs?"

"I did," Kaia said. She knelt next to the fire and held her fingers to it.

Nolen bit his lip, looking uncertain.

"That's how I knew what to do. I could hear the spring talking to me. What I said was what it was telling me. I just know that there were ancient souls in there. Prophecies happened in the old stories... if the spring gave Raven Ancient magic...." Kaia trailed off.

Raven retreated to the back of their shelter to kneel next to Penelope. "Penelope says I've turned into a gorgon, like in the old stories."

Finnegan remained silent through all this discussion, and it occurred to Herja that it wasn't good for him to hear it. Even if he was technically their prisoner, he could also gather information against them.

She got to her feet and grabbed the book bag. "Is this empty now?"

Raven nodded at her.

"Good." Herja marched over to Finnegan. "Take your medications and get into the bag, or just get into the bag. Your choice."

Finnegan lifted his bound hands. "Am I allowed to have these off?"

"You can stick your hands back out once you're in the bag," Herja replied, keeping her voice cold.

As much as she hated being in this position, what else were they meant to do? His constant attacks on them had swallowed up any goodwill Finnegan may have had once upon a time.

Finnegan quietly took the tea Wickham offered him and the rest of the mint camphor. He didn't protest as he crawled awkwardly into the book bag. Herja untied his hands, then secured the mouth of the bag.

"He won't stay warm in there," Kaia said, though her expression said she knew why it had to be done.

"And we can't continue to give him any chances to get the jump on us," Nolen said. He looked up and met Herja's eyes. An understanding passed through them; they'd keep watch tonight to ensure Finnegan didn't escape.

In the meantime, they were all cold and soaked through. It wasn't ideal, but Herja tied the bookbag up on one rope to keep it out of the way, then resumed breaking up the barrels. They built a large fire with this wood that warmed whatever side faced it.

"How long have you known you have the magic of prophecy?" Herja asked Raven once everyone was more or less settled.

Raven sighed. "Is that what I have?"

"Sounds to me like you do. Visions at night, plus a gorgon?" Herja shook her head. "What else could it be?"

"Random dreams that mean nothing," Raven said.

Kaia rubbed her eyes. "I know you want to figure this out, Herja, but please... let's just sleep. We're all so tired. We need to rest."

Herja nodded once. She remained quiet as they adjusted themselves to allow the still-unconscious Penelope warmth from the fire.

There was a mystery here, one that needed to be resolved.... But Kaia was right. For tonight, they needed to focus on recovery. Then, tomorrow they needed to get back to camp. They'd find out soon enough if Finnegan's brother really were dead.

# CHAPTER
# TWENTY-SEVEN

PENELOPE WOKE FEELING BETTER than she had since breaking her arm. It sounded as though the storm had finally passed, and though she was still damp, she wasn't so cold. All this time, the bandages wrapped around her remained intact, with that same protective coating Kaia had put on them before they confronted Finnegan.

"It's not raining anymore. I can go find them," Herja whispered.

Penelope opened her eyes. The others were standing near the pile of broken barrels, huddled together.

Everyone except Raven, that was.

Penelope tested out her motor functions, then slowly got to her feet.

"We need to wait for morning," Nolan said. "We don't know the mountain like Raven. And for all we know, they plan to come back. They said they would."

"After everything that's happened?" Herja's voice pitched even lower, and Penelope got the distinct impression she was doing that on purpose so as not to start yelling. "We can't risk it, Nolan. They're stubborn, but I know I can find them."

"You don't have to keep whispering," Penelope said as she tested her balance. Her legs felt steady enough, and the pain in her shoulder was nearly gone. A blessing, but how long would it last?

Her friends all jumped and whirled, which could have been funny if not for the fear in their eyes. When they saw it was her rather than Finnegan, they relaxed. Penelope strode over to them and peered into the night. Water dripped unsteadily from the trees, indicating post-rain droplets.

"Raven's left again?" Penelope asked.

Herja nodded, looking grim. "They said they had to use the bathroom, but they've been gone for half an hour."

"You and I should go look for them," Penelope said.

She looked around for a loose light stone, but finding nothing, she stepped out from their shelter. The sky was clear, and a near-full moon lit the mountainside. Good. It was enough to work their way some distance and then to return.

Nolan was concerned about them leaving, but once Kaia and Wickham both cast spells over the two to help them find Raven, they headed out.

"You know what I'm looking forward to when we get back to the Institute?" Penelope asked as the chill seeped through her damp clothes.

"Food? Hot water? A trained healer?" Herja guessed.

"All of the above," Penelope agreed. Then, she asked quietly, "Did you know Raven blames themself for you never being adopted?"

Herja's head turned toward her, but Penelope couldn't see her expression in the patch of shadow they walked in.

"No," she finally said.

The two girls found Raven quickly. They stood in a small clearing, and the trees bent from the storms. The sky was bright and clear, the moon washing the land in silver light while the stars twinkled and danced. Northern lights played out over the sky, painting the velvet darkness with hues of green, violet, and blue...

Much like Herja's dragon, now that Penelope thought of it. She initially thought Herja's ombre shades were like water, but this was a much more apt description.

"Raven," Herja called out, striding into the clearing.

Raven stiffened and pulled their face veil back on before they turned. "You really shouldn't go sneaking up on a gorgon, Herja."

"We don't know for certain that's what you are," Herja replied.

Penelope had to roll her eyes at that. "I'm pretty sure that's not the point, Herja."

Herja shot her an annoyed look.

But Penelope ignored her friend this time, focusing instead on Raven. "You need to stop running off like this... you should know that we'd follow."

Raven turned to the two, their face covered once more. "I suppose that's true enough. You are all so stubbornly persistent."

"And you aren't?" Herja demanded as they stopped, the three standing under the stars.

Raven laughed. They sounded lighter than they had any time Penelope had spoken with them before. "That's true, too."

"Darn right it is," Herja muttered.

Her voice was laced with exhaustion, and Penelope touched her shoulder with her uninjured arm. Herja tensed a little but turned to her with a questioning expression.

"Are you going to come back to camp?" Penelope asked Raven.

"I plan to, yes. I just saw the lights, and they were so beautiful... I wanted to look at them clearly without risking anyone else." Raven spread their hands wide. "In hindsight, I should have told you what I was doing."

Penelope moved closer, turning her face to the sky. The northern lights were reaching out from one end of the sky to the others. "They are beautiful. I bet they have a magic in them that we don't know yet."

It struck her suddenly how things had changed. She started this year hearing rumors about the new springs and being adamant there were no other forms of magic. And yet, now she wondered how much more magic was out there that they were completely unaware of.

The three of them stood silently for a long time, staring at the changing lights. Eventually, Herja pushed her black hair from her face.

"The others are going to be worried about us. I should head back," she said.

Penelope nodded. "If it's okay, I'd like to stay out here for a little while longer."

"Are you sure?" Herja pointed at her shoulder.

"I'm sure. It's feeling much better after my sleep".

"It looks worse than ever. If it's feeling better, that could be a sign of nerve damage," Herja said, worried.

Raven answered, "You slept for a few hours, Herja. Wickham and Kaia have been pouring a lot of spells into her. So, it's less likely nerve damage and more that their healing spells have worked."

Herja let out a sigh of relief. "All right, then. That makes sense. And you two will come back to camp soon?"

"Yes," Raven replied.

"Then... I guess there's only one thing left: to ask if you really think it's your fault that I was never adopted?" Herja straightened, then glanced guiltily at Penelope.

"It's all right," Penelope said quickly, recognizing Herja's expression.

They were tired and overwhelmed, meaning their natural filters were at their lowest points. No doubt Herja wouldn't be able to sleep or relax now that she knew about Raven's self-proclaimed guilt.

Raven sighed raggedly. "Isn't it?"

"I can't imagine how it is," Herja replied.

"You and I were up for adoption together. My parents were thinking about adopting both of us, but because of my condition, they decided only to take me." Remorse weighed Raven's voice down. "If they hadn't picked me—"

"Oh, they wouldn't have taken me anyway," Herja interrupted.

Penelope took a few steps away and turned to face the lights again. This talk deserved at least some privacy.

"Your parents are Marla and Jack, aren't they?" Herja pressed.

"Yes."

"Yeah. That's completely not because of your illness, Raven. I read the records of what happened with them... apparently, every time I saw Jack, I bit him hard enough to make him bleed and tried to kick

Marla every time she smiled at me. I was a little demon toward them...
it's my own fault."

Raven was quiet.

Penelope turned back to the two of them. "Maybe now that you're
both older and Herja's outgrown her tendencies to attack people," she
couldn't help but chuckle, "the two of you will talk to them about it. It's
unfair to you, Raven, to carry this guilt around."

"But I'm sure it's my fault," Raven said slowly. "And I'm a year older.
Wouldn't I remember these things?"

"I have the records to prove it," Herja replied with a shrug.

Penelope rejoined them. "Memories like to play tricks on us. So, it's
quite possible that you didn't see what was happening behind the
scenes, and you interpreted your adoption a certain way. Have you
actually ever talked to your parents about this?"

"No," Raven admitted.

"You should."

Herja rubbed her eyes. "I really do need to go back and let the
others know all is well... you're not going to run off again, are you,
Raven?"

Raven shook their head. "No. I'm not going anywhere, not when I
know what persistent bloodhounds you lot are."

Herja laughed. "Good!" Then she opened her arms. "May I hug
you?"

"Er..." Raven visibly flinched. "No. I don't think I'm going to be
comfortable with that. Not until I know exactly what change happened
to my body."

Herja nodded as she lowered her arms again. She headed back to
camp, leaving Penelope and Raven alone. Part of Penelope longed to
return to the fire's warmth, too, but she was less trusting than Herja.
She wasn't so sure that Raven *wouldn't* run off.

Raven lifted their hands to the sky, swaying back and forth under
the lights. "It makes me want to dance. I've never really been one for
dancing, but this is so beautiful."

The other teen's movements were graceful as they spun. Their
hands flowed in circles as the draping of cloth around them spun out

around them. Penelope once more found herself wishing to see Raven's face.

Not just to read their emotions this time, however. She wanted to see what they looked like. What color were their eyes? What shape was their nose?

"Your parents will be happy to get you back home," Penelope said.

Raven lowered their hands. "I think they will be."

"You think?"

Raven let out a ragged sigh. "It's difficult to explain. Sometimes I don't feel like I belong, even with those who love me... I'm not sure there is any place where I belong. And now it feels like that's only become more certain. Where can I go when I'm like this?"

A shiver ran down Penelope's spine. "I know that feeling. Of not belonging even with the people you love and who love you. Ever since I became a dragon, I've been feeling myself getting more and more distant from my family."

"Are they human?" Raven asked.

"No. My mother's a witch. My dad, brother, and sister are all dragons. But nothing has gone according to my plans since I drank from the Silver Springs." Penelope held her one hand out to Raven. "I don't want to think about it—let's dance."

And so they did. Raven took her hand, and they spun and danced below the flowing lights. Penelope allowed her fears to dissipate, singing aloud to give them music to dance to. The two leaped over the ground, bowed, and spun on their toes. The lights grew brighter overhead, as though each leap brought the stars closer.

Eventually, Penelope slowed. She allowed herself to sink to the ground, laughing as Raven collapsed next to her. Despite the chilly night, she was warmed from head to toe from their dancing.

"The others really are going to be worried now," Raven sighed. "But I—what's that?"

Penelope lifted her head. Fine silvery threads wound around Raven's fingers, looping in lovely shimmering tones. They crossed the space between them and Penelope, winding around Penelope's hands, too.

Star threads.

The breath left Penelope's lungs. These were star threads. That meant...

But how?

"I... I..." Penelope awkwardly pushed herself to a sitting position. "I don't understand. These are star threads. They form between fated mates during the matching ceremony. But... but..."

Raven twisted their hands back and forth, the shimmering threads glinting with the glow of the northern lights. "Does this mean... we're a fated pair?"

"I don't know."

It felt like they were, but it seemed impossible. Penelope went through the ceremony last year. She had accepted that she didn't have a mate. So how was she connected to Raven now?

Carefully, she detangled herself from the threads as Raven did the same.

"I don't think we should tell anyone," Penelope said in a low voice. "Not yet. I don't want people to be distracted... we have to figure out how to get you back to your previous form first."

Raven nodded solemnly.

Penelope got to her feet, and the two of them wound the star threads, then stowed them in Raven's cloak. They headed back to the others silently. Penelope's mind raced—how was this even possible?

# CHAPTER
# TWENTY-EIGHT

THE GROUP STRUCK out at first light, and it wasn't long after they hit the main trail back down the mountain that Xena, Jalene, Odele, and Adina found them. Xena let out a whoop and rushed to them. Kaia laughed at his exuberance, or maybe the sheer relief of not being alone in this anymore.

Odele gave Nolan a stern look as the two groups came together. "You should have told me you were leaving."

Kaia glanced at her mate, who was grinning at his twin. "Yes, I should have. I've got a lot to tell you, though. You're gonna love it."

"I doubt it," Odele said, folding her arms, but Kaia saw a grin tugging her lip.

Kaia hugged each of their classmates, expressing relief at seeing them all. "Jalene, Adina, can you help us with Pen? She broke her shoulder—maybe twice—and Wick and I are exhausted. Do you have anything to spare to give her some pain relief?"

Adina stepped forward. "Yes, I think so. What sort of pain relief have you been focusing on?"

"Just block the pain," Penelope said. "Don't try to heal it. I have a feeling that things are all out of place."

Adina nodded, and as she lowered her hands to Penelope's shoulder, Kaia turned to Xena. He was the most enormous dragon in their year. "Can you take a turn carrying the bookbag? Careful, it's got Finnegan in it."

"Finnegan?" Adina repeated, her head whipping around.

"That jerk that attacked us in the Silent Marshes?" Jalene demanded. She glared at the bookbag with distaste.

Kaia noted that none of their classmates had said anything to Raven, though they kept shooting curious looks at the newcomer. Herja opened her mouth, but Kaia intervened. "It's a long story. Let's get back to camp, and then we'll explain everything. And this is Raven. They're a friend of Herja's from the orphanage."

She glanced at the others, Pen, Herja, Wick, and Nolan. They all gave her small nods, letting her know they didn't mind her taking control of the situation.

Good, because Kaia wanted to get back to camp more than anything.

"And it'll be faster to get back down the mountain than up it since the mountain won't be fighting us anymore," Herja added.

Odele frowned, then nodded. "I thought something was wrong."

"Like I said, you're going to love it," Nolan repeated.

Kaia was just happy that they could have backup now. Somehow this, even more than having Finnegan, a passive prisoner, finally said they were over the worst of it.

Fortunately, their fellow students had extra clothing so that everyone could change into dry clothes. Kaia's was a little too snug, especially around the bust, but being free from the incessant dampness was well worth it.

Further down the mountain, they met Icarus, Lena, Victor, and Vera. At this point, Victor and Icarus insist they use the blankets they packed and some large branches from the forest to make a stretcher for Penelope. She grumbled about it but relented soon enough.

"You know what I'm looking forward to most?" Wickham said once they were picking their way down the slippery trail again.

"A bath?" Odele offered, wrinkling her nose.

"Access to more medication?" Herja guessed.

Wickham laughed, the sound bright and carefree. "It was a rhetorical question!"

Both of the dragons blushed and ducked their heads.

"A bath and more medication both sound good, though," Kaia teased. She waved a hand in front of her face. "I bet we all smell!"

Vera nodded sagely.

"What I'm looking forward to most," Wickham said with a roll of his eyes, "is a good, hot meal and then two or three days' worth of sleep."

The thought of food made Kaia's mouth water and her stomach grumble.

At this, Adina pulled out some jerky and other snacks from her pack to pass to the 'missing' students. They even took a small break to pass food and a fresh waterskin to Finnegan. He hadn't caused them any trouble on the journey down the mountain, which could mean he was sick or biding his time.

*Or,* Kaia thought with a wince, *he really is mourning his brother.*

Once slightly lower, Icarus borrowed Kaia's wand to send a few magical flares. After that, it was only a short while before a handful of adult dragons found them.

"Row!" Herja shouted when the professor's glittering black dragon landed. They shifted to their natural form as Herja raced forward.

Kaia's jaw nearly dropped as Herja threw herself into a hug. Though she knew Herja was close to Professor Farrow, she hadn't realized how affectionate Herja was. This was the same sort of hug that she would have rushed to give her mother or father if they were here.

"You four always have to have drama, don't you?" Professor Farrow groused as they gently patted Herja's back. Their eyes narrowed on Nolan. "And I see you're also corrupting who I thought was the most level-headed dragon of your year."

Nolan looked puzzled, but Kaia had to laugh. "You bet! He's my fated mate. What do you expect?"

She twined her hand into Nolan's and gave him a toothy grin.

Odele nodded once. "Teasing," she muttered under her breath.

Farrow and the other dragons checked on Penelope and decided she was in good enough shape to fly back. It was the quickest route, after all. Each of the adults carried two of the teens on their backs. It wasn't so much flying back to camp as gliding, but it was still an immense relief to be off her feet.

Once they were at camp, the five students were given a hot meal, while Raven insisted on the privacy of their own tent. They murmured something to Penelope before they left.

Professor Farrow turned to Penelope. "Let's get you to the medical tent. You can eat there."

"I'd rather stay here and explain about Raven," Penelope said staunchly.

"You can explain while you're being treated. That shoulder is in bad shape," the professor rumbled, their normally stoic expression creased with worry.

Penelope opened her mouth to argue, then closed it in a hurry. From the sudden pallor on her face, she had a feeling that the last spells had just worn off, and the pain hit her full force once again. She nodded meekly, and one of the other adults ushered her away.

"Finnegan came after us again," Kaia said, gesturing toward the bookbag. "We have him in there, but he's sick. He's going to need medical attention, too."

Professor Farrow picked up the bag. "How did he end up here?"

Kaia shook her head, suddenly exhausted. "I don't know. He wanted to drink from the springs."

"Eat," Professor Farrow urged, patting her shoulder. "We'll take care of this."

Kaia nodded once. She sat heavily and ate. After a few bites, her exhaustion became all the more apparent. After days of running on stress, they were finally safe...

And with any luck, she'd never have to see Finnegan again.

HERJA WAS reluctant to talk about Raven and what happened with all the adults around, so she asked Row for time, just the two of them, to talk about it. Row nodded.

"I'll walk you to your tent, but you really need to sleep. You look like you're about to fall over," they said gently.

Herja wrinkled her nose as she (unsuccessfully) fought back a yawn. "But there's too much to talk about. I don't want to betray Raven's trust, but something happened to them. It's not safe to walk in on them without warning."

How were the adults going to treat Raven? Raven themselves had been convinced this was a curse on them for drinking from the spring. But the ancient sword that Finnegan had, and the voices Kaia heard in the fountain... there had to be something else going on, right?"

"You need sleep. Penelope already told us that Raven has had something happen to them," Row said when Herja protested. "We know they have the magic to turn living creatures into stone."

Herja winced but nodded. "And the Institute will help them, right?"

Row sighed. "Right now, there isn't much we can do until we've heard everything from all of you. And we can't hear from all of you until you have had a good rest. Now go to bed."

"But Raven will get help, won't they?" Herja asked, a tight feeling coming to her chest. "Even though they've become a gorgon?"

"Yes. Doesn't matter if they're a gorgon, a manticore, or anything else." Row smiled at Herja reassuringly. "They will get help. I promise you that."

They walked with Herja toward Herja's tent, but when Herja spied the new tent, no doubt where Raven was, she changed directions.

"Herja," Row said with a frown.

"They're my friend, and I need to talk to them. If it were your friend, you'd do the same," Herja added with a half-glare, daring Row to argue with her.

Row sighed but nodded again. "Don't stay talking too long; I need to go to the medical tent and see what's happening with Pen and Finnegan. Make sure you get back to your tent to sleep before too long, okay?"

Herja nodded as they came to a stop outside Raven's tent. Row headed off, and Herja took a deep breath.

"Raven?" she called. "Can I come in?"

After a moment's silence, Raven called back. "Yes."

Herja ducked in, rubbing her neck as she did so. She was exhausted but wanted to check in on her friend before she slept.

Raven was sitting on a cot, a clean veil over their face. Unlike the last one, which looked like a raggedy funeral shroud, it was embroidered with flowers along the lower end and draped over their face like a regular veil would be. A simple leather band circled their head, keeping it in place.

"Wow. You look like the oracles of old," Herja said as she let the tent flap fall behind her.

"Do I?" Raven asked.

"Yeah. At least, you look the way I always imagined them. I wonder if that's what Kaia heard at the springs... the voices of the oracles from ancient times." Herja tucked her hands behind her back, averting her eyes now. "You know... I'm not that great with talking and emotions."

Raven laughed softly. "I'm not sure anyone is."

"I'm particularly bad at it. But I just wanted to let you know it's not your fault. Why I'm not adopted, even if Marla and Jack decided they couldn't care for the both of us because of your illness, that was their choice. It's not your fault."

"It feels like my fault."

Herja shook her head. "Well, feelings lie. They kind of suck that way."

Raven laughed again, this time sounding more like they meant it. "They do, don't they?"

"And I wanted to let you know, I'll stay with you as much as possible," Herja added. "Over the summer, if you stay at the Institute, so will I."

Raven was quiet for a moment. Then sighed. "Thank you, Herja. And as much as I would like that, you can't."

"I can, too. I can—"

"Wickham needs you," Raven interrupted. "And I won't be alone, anyway. Penelope has already decided she'll stay with me."

Penelope? Herja's tense muscles relaxed. Penelope would be able to take care of the situation. She'd be better able to push for answers without angering the researchers.

"Oh. Well, I can still stay with you," Herja offered.

Raven shook their head. "Wickham needs you. And from your look, you need sleep—and so do I. Goodnight, Herja."

Herja recognized the 'please leave and let me sleep' that Raven was too polite to stay. She nodded once and headed out again. It wasn't until she was in her tent, crawling into bed, that it occurred to her... was Raven's declaration that Wickham needed her prophecy, or something else?

Then her head hit the pillow, and Herja was asleep at once.

# CHAPTER
# TWENTY-NINE

*SEVERAL MONTHS Later*

It was the end of yet another school year at the Institute. Kaia smoothed out the gingham dress she'd sewn after returning to the Institute to finish classes, then double-checked to ensure she had all her belongings.

It had been yet another eventful semester. She was starting to think there might be something to the idea that their year was cursed somehow. Nobody else had to deal with the stuff they had.

Fortunately, despite Herja's fears, they had still managed to complete their coursework. A satisfied smile spread over her face as she let her fingers pass over the roc-feather quill in her spell book kit. After their arduous trek to that magic springs and all the trouble Finnegan brought, getting to the old roc nests to collect a feather hadn't been all that difficult.

She tucked it into the kit, the emerald rattleback skin she'd collected in her first year, and the pages made from the Phoenix Ginkgo last year.

Next year, they'll be collected ink from a kraken. And then their quests would be over.

"Are you ready to go?" Penelope asked from behind her.

Kaia turned. The damage done to Penelope's shoulder had been severe; so bad, in fact, that she was still receiving physical therapy for it. But she was getting better, and Penelope told her it didn't even hurt anymore.

"Yeah. I'm about ready to go. I already said goodbye to the others. I was hoping to find you before I had to head out." Kaia crossed the room and pulled Penelope into a tight hug. "Thank you. I know it has to be exhausting being the lynchpin for our group."

Penelope made a half-strangled, half-amused noise. "Yeah, but who else is going to do it?"

Kaia stepped back. "I don't know. I guess that's why we need you, eh?"

"Guess so." Penelope glanced at Kaia's suitcase. "So, did you and Nolen decide what you're doing for the summer? Is it going to be a split between your families like last year?"

Right. With all of Penelope's physical therapy, she hadn't been around as much. Kaia smacked her own forehead. "Ugh! I forgot to tell you. I'm sorry—no, we're not. That is, we are, but not to start with."

Penelope raised a single fiery eyebrow. "Well, that's clear as mud."

"Nolen and I were invited to join Icarus's parents as part of the royal ambassador party to Odentia when King Sydney goes to congratulate the new queen and talk about what will happen with Finnegan." Kaia had to repress a shiver as she thought of it. She'd never left Eldavon before. "Afterward, we're going to spend a couple of weeks with each other's families."

Penelope stared at her with a dropped jaw. "You're going to Odentia?"

Kaia nodded.

"About Finnegan?"

"Yes. I know, I should have told you. I guess everything just happened so fast...." Kaia returned to her suitcase and shut it. "I talked myself out of going a dozen times. But it feels like the right choice."

"Is Finnegan going, too?" Penelope asked, clearly still in shock.

"Not that I'm aware of. Last I heard, he was being held in a custom prison in the Golden Forest." The Chameleon Sprites could keep him contained even if he tried to escape again. "But since apparently he and I have a... connection? I guess? King Sydney believes it will be good for me to address the new queen to relate my experiences."

Kaia finished closing her suitcase as she reflected on the journey that had brought her here. When they graduated, Nolan wanted to work with the sea in some capacity, but Kaia hadn't thought too much about it.

She had a lot of skill in languages, though. Perhaps they could be some sort of sailor ambassadors. Or maybe have nothing to do with politics at all... it was a heavy responsibility, after all.

"I think this is one area I can help with," she finally said, turning back to Penelope. "And I must admit, I'm curious about this new queen. She's only supposed to be our age."

Penelope's nose wrinkled. "Oh, that's way too young! How is she supposed to take care of everything?"

"I don't know. But I want to find out."

Penelope nodded. "And Finnegan... what will you be asking for?"

"I don't know. I hate the idea of anyone being in the Odentia prisons if they're really what I've heard. On the other hand, it could be that Finnegan was treated extra badly because his brother was manipulating him." Kaia shrugged and spread her hands. "I guess that's just one more thing that I'll be finding out about."

Penelope hugged her again.

Kaia hugged her back. "I'll tell you everything when we get back next semester."

"You better."

"And what about you? Are you really staying at the Institute over the summer?" Kaia asked.

"I'm staying with Raven," Penelope said somewhat cryptically.

"Good. They've got a hard road ahead of them." Kaia smiled, but her gut twisted. She couldn't help but wonder if she had made a mistake in burying the second spring.

The Earth must have given them another chance at magic for a reason. At the very least, it might have provided answers for Raven.

"Your carriage is going to be waiting," Penelope said, nodding toward the door. "Have a safe trip."

"Thanks."

Kaia picked up her suitcase and headed out. Regardless of what could have been done differently, she could only think about the future now. *Take it one step at a time and figure out where I'm going when I have sturdy ground again.*

❈

HERJA LOOKED over the latest test results, her heart sinking low. Inconclusive. Why had everything been inconclusive? Not neurotypical enough to be neurotypical. Not neurodivergent enough to be neurodivergent. So where did it leave her?

With a sigh, she put the papers on Row's desk. "More of the same," she said.

"I'm sorry. I know it's difficult," Row said.

Herja nodded, annoyed despite herself. Odele had gotten her results back with answers. She was on the autism spectrum, and Herja had already overhead her telling Nolen that it was such a relief to know that she wasn't just weird... her brain worked differently.

"Maybe it just means there is more research and learning that needs to be done in this area," Herja said. "Maybe it's because we as a society are changing so rapidly in our understanding of how the brain works; we just don't have the information we need."

Row nodded. "I'd agree with you there, for sure. I'm not sure that it's even all that fair to consider 'neurotypical' and 'neurodivergence' as a strict binary, either... but then, I never did buy into binaries."

They winked at her, which eased Herja's frustration. "Thank you for trying to help me with this, at least. Not having answers is one thing, but it's bearable. I know it's not because I'm slipping through the cracks so much as... there just aren't answers for my particular case."

"Of course. In his last letter, Bryce mentioned he was worried about the non-answers being too frustrating for you. So, if you need to talk to anyone, I'm here, there are the councilors... And Wickham," Row added, softer.

Herja flinched. No, she hadn't been telling Wick about all this. Not yet at least. "We've been busy, and he's worrying himself in knots over his little brothers."

"That doesn't mean your emotional needs should be invisible," Row said.

"That's exactly what it means. You don't shovel dirt onto someone who's already struggling to hold themself up," Herja replied.

Row smirked at her. "Except that's not at all what I'm saying. You can share with Wickham what is happening in your life without making it his problem to solve, you know."

"How?"

"It's as simple as 'Wickham. Lately, I've been very frustrated with the lack of answers I've gotten from seeking a diagnosis. I know you have a lot on your plate, and I don't want to overburden you, but you should know. I'll work with the school counselors, Mr. Bryce, and Professor Farrow on it.' See? Simple."

Herja frowned at her professor. They might act like it was that simple, but it wasn't. Knowing Wickham, he'd just add worry over her onto his over-piled plate and make everything all the worse.

"I can see I haven't convinced you," Row said.

"Not really. But I'm done trying to seek a diagnosis for right now. I've got enough 'inconclusive' tests back to know that I'm somewhere that doesn't quite fit, and I have to accept it's not bad." Herja twisted her hands in her lap.

No, it wasn't a bad thing. But it certainly felt bad for someone like her, who liked to have clear, definitive answers.

Row nodded; their face was sympathetic. "Did you have anything else you wanted to talk about?"

"Should I?" Herja instantly asked.

Then she flinched. She did. She hadn't come to Row's office looking for anything to do with the diagnosis. She took a deep breath. That was a distraction because she didn't want the vulnerability of what she came here for.

"Professor Delphine says that you're an orphan, too."

"Yes. My biological parents were killed in an earthquake when I was very young." Row's expression didn't falter. "Did you want to hear about my adoption story?"

Herja shook her head. "I mean, yes. But not now. What I want to know is... in your opinion, one orphan to another, am I too old to be adopted?"

Row's silver eyes widened. "No. But I thought you didn't want to be adopted."

"I didn't. Or at least, I thought I didn't." Herja rubbed her forehead, trying to put her thoughts in order. She had spent so long analyzing herself that her feelings had grown distant... and yet speaking about this aloud brought them back up.

"Do you want to talk about it?"

"I think I fought so hard against being adopted because I thought I wasn't adoptable for some reason... or maybe it felt like I was betraying my parents, wanting another mom and dad." Herja stared at Row's desk, not daring to look them in the eye. "But..."

Row waited patiently for her to continue.

"But not being adopted hurts, too. I hear the others talking about their families, and I feel like I'm missing something." Herja lifted her head, chewing her lip as she did so. "So, I wanted to know if it's even possible."

"Of course it is. Lots of families adopt older children."

"But in two years, I'll graduate from the Institute and be an adult. What's the point?"

Row shook their head. "Family doesn't stop the moment you turn eighteen, Herja. You are adoptable."

"All right. Well. I guess that's something to think about next semester, then." Herja stood, gathering her papers again.

"Why not over the summer?"

"Wick needs me," Herja replied. "I don't know why... but he does. So, I can't think of myself for the summer. Only him."

Row looked... sad, almost, as they sighed. "That's not how this is supposed to work, Herja."

"But it's the way I work." Herja turned on her heel and marched away, not daring to look back for fear she'd tell Row what she really wanted.

*I want to be your daughter.*

# CHAPTER

# THIRTY

WICKHAM SIGHED in relief as he approached the little swing atop the hill on the path to the pond. The tension in his shoulders eased as he saw Herja sitting there, writing in her notebook. He really shouldn't have convinced himself that she had left without saying goodbye.

As he approached, she looked up and shut the notebook. Was this her journal, her study notes, or her novel? He almost wished he didn't have to disturb her.

"Hey," he called as he reached her. "Do you have some time to talk?"

Herja gestured to the swing. "Of course."

Wickham sat and let out a sigh. He'd been running around all over the Institute looking for her. "Soooo... I have a favor to ask of you."

"What is it?"

Wickham wrapped his hand around one of the warm chains holding the swing. "You know that Donnelly and Rhett will be making the trip to the Silver Springs this summer, right?"

Herja's lips twitched. "No, I think I forgot about that."

"Hardy har har," Wickham drawled but grew serious again quickly. "I'm worried that Odentia will try to intervene again."

"They haven't come after any of the children since our year, and the Odentia Crown has been very explicit in saying Finnegan acted alone."

Wickham shook his head. "I know. But logic isn't helping. I'm scared for them. I got permission to be at the palace as part of the healers for this coming year."

Herja nodded, a pinch in her brow.

Wickham was hesitant to ask her, knowing that these fears were silly. Besides, she had so much on her plate with her quest for a diagnosis. He chewed his lip as he toed the ground, making them sway back and forth.

"So, you want me to come with you?" Herja finally prompted.

"Yeah," Wickham admitted. "I think having you with me, with your logical straightforwardness, will help a lot."

"You really think so?" Herja asked, her brow creasing further.

Wickham turned to her. "I know I can let my head run away with me sometimes. I get into thinking about all this stuff, and I need someone to snap me out of it. You're really good at that."

"I am?"

"Yes. That's why I said you were." Wickham stuck his tongue out teasingly at her. "But I'll understand if you're too busy."

Herja shook her head, her silver eyes solemn. "I'm not too busy. These are your brothers. You love them very much. And it'll be good for me to have something else to occupy my thoughts. Besides, I should get to know your family as your mate."

Wickham's breath left his lungs at her words. At that moment, he wanted so badly to kiss her. He had to turn away.

She didn't want that. He was not going to ruin their relationship.

"Thank you," he said, and his voice was deeper than usual for some reason.

They sat silently, swaying back and forth for several minutes before Herja cleared her throat.

"Wickham, I feel very vulnerable when I'm around you."

His head came up.

"It's not a bad thing. In fact, it feels... I don't know, it feels good, I guess," Herja said, staring off toward the pond. "I feel vulnerable because I know I can be. I just... I don't want to burden you with my struggles."

Wickham tried to understand what she was saying. "I... I feel the same way. But just know I can see you struggling, and it hurts when you shut me out."

"Right. Just like it hurts me if you shut me out." Her voice was stiff, formal. "So, you should know. I'm not going to seek a diagnosis anymore. But I am thinking about... seeing what I need to do to be adopted."

Wickham processed her words. She never talked that much about her lack of family. If he had had to hazard a guess, he would have thought she didn't care—but clearly, he was wrong.

"Whatever you need me to do, let me know," Wickham told her. "Can I hug you?"

Herja turned to him. "Please."

Wickham embraced his perfect match, hugging her close. A warm feeling spread through his chest. This is precisely what he wanted from his relationship with Herja. For her to confide in him, for him to confide in her.

This was what made them fated mates. And it was precisely what he could count on.

⊱⋅ ⋅⊰

AFTER THE HUSTLE and bustle of students leaving the campus had died down, Penelope found a peaceful quiet descended on the Institute. She had stayed here over winter breaks before, but she had never stayed during the summer.

She liked it. The quiet. Wandering these ancient hallways, imaging all the history that happened here.

She missed her family, but they would stop in occasionally. Julie and Trace were talking about coming for a few weeks, too. Julie wanted to upgrade some of her learning, and Trace would come with her with little Reuel; he must be getting so big now!

Penelope entered the dormitory to find Raven with their luggage. Penelope's brows arched.

"Aren't you and your parents living in the guest quarters?" Penelope asked.

Raven turned. Today, their face veil was brown with thick lines of embroidered lightning. With the uniform they wore, they cut a very strong and imposing figure.

"Since I'll be enrolled as a student officially next semester, the Headmasters suggested it would be good for me to move into the dorm. Well, they talked about putting me in with the third-years or fifth years next year, but I wanted to be in the same year as you and Herja."

Penelope nodded. They still didn't understand Raven's magic well, but all the adults agreed it was more of a witch-type magic than a dragon-type. So over the summer, the professors would work closely with Raven to bring them up to speed on the various magics the witches already worked.

That was, in between the research, trying to figure out if Raven's human form could be restored.

"I just don't know where I'm supposed to go," Raven said as they gestured to the rooms. "Here are the girls' rooms. The boys' are over there."

Penelope joined Raven in the center of the room, looking back and forth.

"It's just another way this school wasn't built for me," Raven murmured. "I'm not sure what your headmasters are thinking. I'm not a witch. I'm not a dragon. I'm not a girl or a boy. I don't... I don't fit."

"Professor Farrow is also non-binary. We were only divided into girls and boys this year because our years are binary," Penelope said quickly, hoping to make Raven feel better.

Raven sat down on one of the overstuffed armchairs. "I already talked to Professor Farrow about it. They agree that things here are divided into binary roles a bit too much around here."

Penelope sank onto the armrest. She had never seen it like that. It had all just been so... ordinary for her.

"I'm sorry," she said.

Raven lifted one shoulder and let it drop. "Eldavon, as a whole, is very aware of discrepancies and tries to fix them. But that doesn't mean it's perfect. It's frustrating. I know things are changing for the better... but..."

"In the meantime, it's hard to find the place you belong," Penelope finished for them. She let out a sigh. "Yeah. And since it's not something I thought about—"

"It means you've just learned something," Raven interrupted swiftly.

"I was going to say I'm part of the problem."

Raven tilted their face up; Penelope could see the outline of their nose pressed against the face veil. "You as a person are not part of the problem."

Would it be possible to kiss through that veil? Not that Penelope wanted to kiss them... but would it be possible?

Penelope turned away, ashamed of her thoughts. Raven was going through enough; they shouldn't have to deal with these intrusive thoughts either.

"Like I said, though, it is changing," Raven said. "And that's what I try to focus on. As for what room to be in, I think I'd like to share with Herja."

A little bud of jealousy pricked Penelope's heart. "Why not mine?"

"Because it's inappropriate for fated mates to share a bedroom, especially at our age."

Fated mates. Penelope thought of the silvery threads that the two of them had hidden in Penelope's trunk. With so much happening with the research into Raven's powers, the two had decided to keep it a secret for longer.

"You know, I have been struggling with not having a fated mate all year," Penelope said, turning back to Raven. A wry smirk spread over her face. "And now I'm struggling to accept that I have one."

"I understand."

"No, you don't; I spent an entire year thinking that I wasn't given a mate because I was wrong for one," Penelope explained softly. "I thought something was wrong with me."

Raven let out a sharp exclamation. "But there's nothing wrong with you!"

"Well... I haven't internalized that yet," Penelope admitted. She touched her chest above her heart. "I just keep thinking all of this has to have happened for a reason, but how can I be the mate you need me to be?"

"And you don't think I have those same thoughts? I hardly know anything about what fated mates are supposed to be!" Raven threw their hands in the air.

Penelope belted out a laugh. "Good!"

"Good?"

Penelope nodded, continuing to laugh. "Weren't we just saying that it was important for us not to think in binary terms? Well, why should we think in singular terms for fated mates, then?"

Raven leaned back in their chair, laughing with Penelope.

As the two of them put Raven's luggage in the dorm room with Herja's bed, Penelope suddenly remembered the previous year. When the Chameleon Sprites had created a false world with everything she wanted, it included her fated mate.

Even in that world, she couldn't see her mate's face. Could that have been a prophecy? Maybe. Or maybe it was just a coincidence...

It didn't matter.

She had her mate now. And she would find answers for Raven. She would be there for her mate, regardless of the future.

**The End**

If you enjoyed this book, please consider leaving a review on Goodreads, Bookbub or your favorite retailer.

Reviews help me reach new readers.

Read *The Quest for the Kraken's Ink*, the fourth book in the *Defenders of the Realm* series!

*OR*

Read *A Summer of Courage*, the third Fantasy Romance Novella in the *Defenders of the Realm* series!

*OR*
*Have you read the prequel?*
*A Journey to Power*

**Join my Newsletter for writing updates, sales and giveaways!**
**www.mhlebeault.com**